RITE OF ABNEGATION

A NOVEL

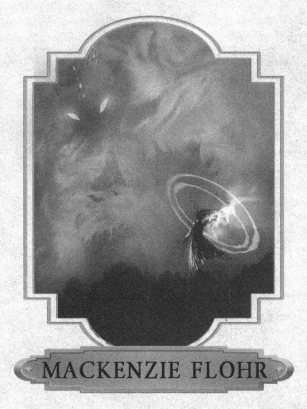

MACKENZIE FLOHR

bhc press

Livonia, Michigan

Edited by Lisa McNeilley and Rebecca Rue

THE RITE OF ABNEGATION
Copyright © 2020 Mackenzie Flohr

This book is a work of fiction. The characters, incidents, and dialogue are drawn from the author's imagination and are not to be construed as real. Any resemblance to actual events or persons, living or dead, is entirely coincidental.

Published by BHC Press

Library of Congress Control Number:
2018931567

ISBN: 978-1-947727-50-2 (Hardcover)
ISBN: 978-1-64397-093-6 (Softcover)
ISBN: 978-1-64397-094-3 (Ebook)

For information, write:
BHC Press
885 Penniman #5505
Plymouth, MI 48170

Visit the publisher:
www.bhcpress.com

Never stop believing in your dream.
Mine came true because of all of *you.*

Thank you for continuing
this journey with me.

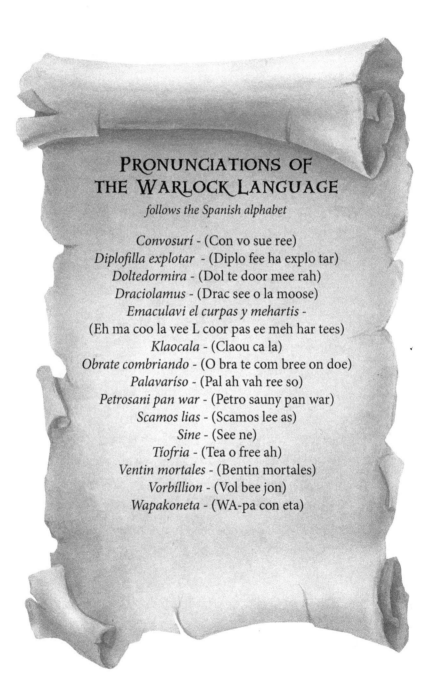

PRONUNCIATIONS OF THE WARLOCK LANGUAGE

follows the Spanish alphabet

Convosurí - (Con vo sue ree)
Diplofilla explotar - (Diplo fee ha explo tar)
Doltedormira - (Dol te door mee rah)
Draciolamus - (Drac see o la moose)
Emaculavi el curpas y mehartis -
(Eh ma coo la vee L coor pas ee meh har tees)
Klaocala - (Claou ca la)
Obrate combriando - (O bra te com bree on doe)
Palavaríso - (Pal ah vah ree so)
Petrosani pan war - (Petro sauny pan war)
Scamos lias - (Scamos lee as)
Sine - (See ne)
Tíofria - (Tea o free ah)
Ventin mortales - (Bentin mortales)
Vorbíllion - (Vol bee jon)
Wapakoneta - (WA-pa con eta)

HOW TO READ ORLYND'S DIALECT

Ah = I	ma = my
Ah'd = I'd	mair = more
Ah'm = I am	n = and
Ah've = I have	nae = not
ain = way	oan = on
ay = of	oor = our
dinnae = don't	tae = to
eywis = these	thair = their
fi = from	thir = there
fir = for	thit = that
gen up = really?	whit = what
git = get	wi = with
goat = got	wid = would
hame = home	wis = was
hudnae = had not	yir = you're
huv = have	yis = you
intae = into	

"It doesn't matter what happens in your life;
what matters is how you choose to react to it."
~ Mackenzie Flohr ~

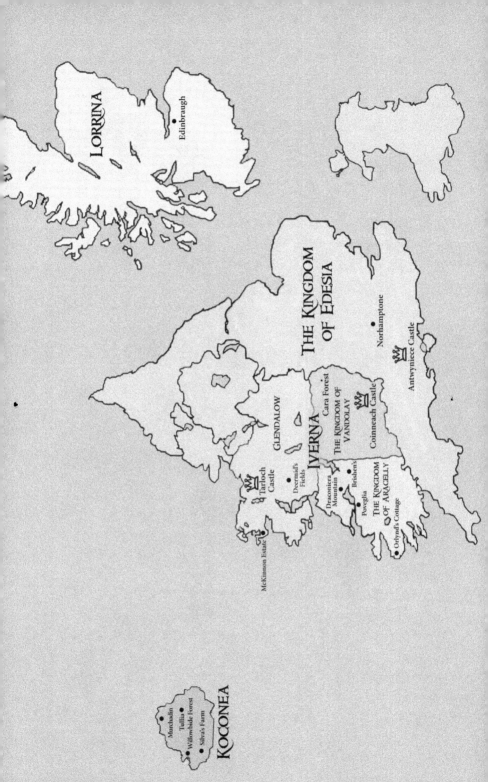

THE
RITE
OF
ABNEGATION

CHAPTER ONE

THE KINGDOM OF ARACELLY
1220 CE

Tell me about the Rite of Wands," the young boy uttered under his breath.

"Not this again. Gearoid, will you please get on with it before our son gives me a headache?" Winifred McKinnon complained.

Gearoid McKinnon stared across the carriage at his twelve-year-old son nervously shuffling his feet. The noise of the horse's hooves overpowered any other sound.

"Mortain," Gearoid began, addressing his son with a bit of a warning. "We have already discussed this. I have informed you of everything I am permitted to."

"Yes, I know," Mortain said, apologetically, wiping his brown bangs out of his eyes. "But, I wish to hear it again! It won't be much longer till we've reached Draconiera Mountain, and I must be prepared for the ceremony. Please, tell me the story of Lord Kaeto?"

Mortain was so distracted by thinking about what was coming that he didn't even look around at the town. He barely noticed when the small, cosy cottages gave way to the close, tightly packed shops of midtown. The many townsfolk busily going about their daily tasks were nothing but ghosts beyond the carriage windows.

"Very well," Gearoid said, sighing heavily. "The Rite of Wands ceremony dates back to ancient times before witches and warlocks existed in Iverna. Plague had swept the land with no cure in sight. Only when all hope seemed to be lost, an invisible gateway to the Neamh Coelum opened."

"The gateway wasn't really invisible, was it?" Mortain interrupted, curious.

"Yes, well, um?" Gearoid stuttered as he searched his mind for the proper answer. "Truth be told, I don't know; I've never seen it in my travels."

"Oh," Mortain said, disappointed.

Gearoid continued, "Lord Kaeto, originating from a magnificent breed of legendary and omniscient telepathic dragons, chose to enter the gate, bringing a cure to save the people of Iverna—along with the secret of magic, which was transmitted onto the survivors residing in the kingdom of Aracelly."

"And that's how magic came to the kingdom!" Mortain grinned.

"Yes," Gearoid said, a bit annoyed. "Magic was a part of Lord Kaeto and thus now a part of the kingdom of Aracelly. However, it could not merely pass from mother and father to child the way curly hair or the ability to run quickly might. First, a child had to be born in the kingdom of Aracelly for the potential for magic to be in them. Being born anywhere else in Iverna, regardless of who their parents are, would exclude them from inheriting the ability to perform magic. Second, that child would have to face an examination of the soul to prove he or she had more than simply the strength to perform magic."

"The Rite of Wands ceremony," Mortain uttered.

"That's correct," Gearoid said. "Lord Kaeto decreed that starting on the twelfth birthday, each was invited to participate. The goal is to be welcomed into the magical community as a full-fledged member. They would see a glimpse into their futures with the right to earn their wands and magical powers if their souls faced the ultimate analysis. How each person endured would determine their destiny. Some participants have gone mad during the Rite of Wands ceremony and thus failed."

"But what if I choose not to be a warlock? What happens then?" Mortain interrupted.

"You most certainly will be a warlock if you don't desire to be declared an outcast the rest of your life!" his mother scolded.

"Now, now, dear. He meant naught from it," Gearoid said, attempting to calm his wife.

"Nonsense! If he wants to bring shame to our family, then so be it. I declare now such a foolish idea would never come from my side of the family. I swear, I sometimes question why my father fancied to marry me to someone of your background so eagerly."

Gearoid sighed, exasperated.

It seemed whenever his wife would become displeased, she used the opportunity to toss insults about his family. She always felt that she had married beneath her station in life and wasn't afraid of reminding him. He turned his attention to his son and smiled at him.

"Whatever shall happen shall be determined during your Rite of Wands. However, if you should not pass, or for some foolish reason decide not to become a warlock, you will be forced to endure the Rite of Abnegation and spend the rest of your life as a magical person without your powers. You shall be stripped of all magical abilities, your wand will be confiscated, and you will be transformed into a Magulia."

"I do not understand. How do you get transformed, Father? Do Magulias look different?"

Gearoid shook his head. "No. They look no different than the ordinary warlock except they have had *Ventin mortales* cast upon them. It is a curse that all warlocks fear, for it can only be spoken from Lord Kaeto's mouth."

"Do we know any Magulias?"

"Of course not," his mother spat out. "We do not associate with those people and we never will!"

"Be silent, woman!" Gearoid said.

"But, why, Mum? What's wrong with being a regular man?"

Gearoid shot his wife a warning glance.

"That's enough for now, Mortain. We've reached the market. The carriage is slowing down. Best to start preparing for boarding the ferry to Draconiera Mountain, yes?"

DRACONIERA MOUNTAIN— THE KINGDOM OF ARACELLY 1220 CE

DRACONIERA MOUNTAIN—renowned for the Rite of Wands ceremony—is located in central Aracelly on an island formed from a tributary of the River Regía. The River Regía diverts with the River Magdalena, forming a circular body of water surrounding the island before connecting again at the market. It is there where witches and warlocks gather, on or after their twelfth birthdays, to board a ferry to their destination together. Mortain looked at the other witches and wizards, many standing beside their parents waiting for the ferry to arrive. He could see that they all seemed as nervous as he himself felt.

Once the ferry docked, Mortain followed his parents toward Draconiera Mountain. He was taken aback at how impossibly large the mountain was this close up. Mortain had seen the forest-covered mountain many times before but it was always from afar. The peak, which always seemed to be shrouded in misty clouds, was completely hidden from view on this day. Gently guided by his father, Mortain entered into the mountain. He began to cough only a few minutes after entering.

"Careful, Son," his father cautioned. "Your brain is deceiving you to believe you are suffocating. Breathe as you normally would."

Mortain took in another deep breath, feeling the hot air fill his nostrils. It felt as if someone was purposely wanting to set his lungs on fire. "It's so hot and the air is so heavy," he whined.

"Yes, that is true. However, it is necessary to keep the environment inside the mountain warmer in order to maintain Lord Kaeto's temperature. It will be quite unpleasant until your body adjusts." As they walked farther away from the entrance, the light became dimmer and dimmer. Gearoid turned to his wife. "We shall require light to lead the way through the mountain from this point forward. Would you, my dear, do us the honours?"

Winifred reached into her robe, pulling out an ebony wand with a crocoite crystal connected at the shaft.

"*Scamos lias!*" she chanted, lighting the path before them.

Mortain parted his lips, allowing a small gasp to escape. For as far as his eyes could see before them, there was a seemingly endless pathway. The ceiling, towering far above them, had stalactite hanging from it. The stalactites had every colour imaginable running through them. Water dripped down upon anyone who happened to be walking below, and the rock walls seemed to gleam with the same orange hue as the crystal on his mum's wand. In the near distance, he could also hear what sounded like water rushing from below.

After following the path for several minutes, Mortain broke the silence.

"Blimey, is that water I hear?" he asked, attempting to distract himself from the dread that was growing deep within him.

"Sorry?" his father said, trying to recall the location of the sound. "Ah, yes, there's a waterfall not too far away from here. Be careful not to stand too close to the edge of the pathway, my son. You wouldn't wish to fall. If I recall correctly, there's a hot spring somewhere underneath."

Mortain looked down and could see that the pathway seemed to be separated from the walls in some spots with steam rising from below through the openings.

"It would be a rather unfortunate way to die," Mortain said.

DRACONIERA MOUNTAIN—
THE KINGDOM OF ARACELLY
1220 CE

"WHAT IS this place?" Mortain asked as the doors to the anteroom opened. Inside was a circular room with the same rock structure as the rest of the mountain. Two torches were positioned adjacent to the doors, leading toward the stage for the Rite of Wands ceremony. The air felt extra stuffy with half of the room already filled with young witches and warlocks and their parents seated on the many stone benches, anxiously awaiting their turn. *They must have come on an earlier ferry.*

Mortain looked at the faces of the others waiting to be summoned. He locked eyes with a young warlock. His face was pale, eyes wide with fright, and Mortain was certain he could see beads of sweat on his forehead. The young warlock glanced at his father who was seated next to him. His father gave a reassuring nod, but it did not seem to help him relax.

Blimey! Mortain thought to himself, *I hope I don't look that scared.*

"This," Gearoid said, gazing around the room for a less crowded area, "is where you'll wait until it's your time to participate."

"Oh," Mortain answered, letting out a small breath to help calm his nerves.

"Come along, Mortain, keep up." Winifred gestured, proceeding toward an empty space in the opposite corner.

Mortain was drawn to a group of witches gathered together. As he passed them, he noticed one of the witches abruptly gasp.

Cecilia, who Mortain had known since childhood, looked over at her friend Esmeralda, her expression showing excited apprehension.

"What happened? Did you hear him?" he overheard her friend ask eagerly.

The witch nodded, a smile forming with her lips. "Yes, I heard him say my name," Cecilia said.

"Yay!" Esmeralda cheered, clapping her hands together between moments of jumping up and down.

Cecilia turned to her parents. "Did you hear that? He called my name!"

"What is she going on about?" Mortain asked his mother.

"Never mind, Mortain," Winifred scolded. "It is rude to listen to other people's conversations without first being invited."

"But I really wish to understand!" Mortain countered. "Who said her name? I heard nothing!"

"It would appear the witch heard the voice of no one other than Lord Kaeto himself," Gearoid answered, watching the witch's friend playfully shove her toward the entrance.

A loud creaking echoed across the room, and the ground shook underneath their feet. Two tall wooden doors opened up to a pathway of complete darkness.

"I can hear him," Cecilia said, turning to Gearoid who was standing near the doorway. "He's telling me to step inside."

"Go on then," Gearoid said. "It is best not to keep him waiting. Simply remember to be confident and show him your abilities."

Cecilia gazed from Gearoid over to Winifred and Mortain, nodding. "Thank you, sir," she said. She took in a deep breath and walked into the darkness.

As they all watched until the doors closed behind her, Mortain wondered when it would be his turn.

✕ ✕ ✕

MORTAIN AND his parents had been seated on one of the benches for quite some time and Mortain was becoming fidgety.

"What is taking so long? We have been here too long!" Mortain whined. He felt that he had been waiting for an eternity. The anteroom, which had originally been filled close to capacity, was now nearly empty.

"Patience, patience, my boy," Gearoid insisted, though he was struggling with his own urge to get the rite underway.

"But I have been waiting for hours!" Mortain complained, wiping the sweat from his forehead with the sleeve of his robe. "Maybe Lord Kaeto doesn't want me to become a warlock. Maybe he thinks I'm not good enough!"

"Now, now, Mortain," Gearoid scolded. "There shall be none of that. You are my son. Therefore, that makes you more than worthy of becoming a warlock."

"But, what if it's true, Father?" Mortain continued anxiously. "What if I'm unable to perform magic? What if we came all this way only to be tricked? You and Mum always said that what I do reflects on you. What if I'm destined to become a…a…a Magulia?"

"MORTAIN MCKINNON!"

Mortain gasped, standing abruptly. His body trembled as he looked around the room, trying to determine the source of the voice. He felt his cheeks blush as he contemplated whether he was going mad. "Who?" he said between gasps. "Who said that? Was that…?"

Even though he had seen the others' reactions and knew how they were summoned, Mortain was surprised by the force of the voice in his head. He felt as though his name thundered and rumbled through the air of the anteroom.

"What did you hear, my son?" Gearoid questioned, trying his best to hide his excitement.

"Argh!"

The sound of thunder smashed against the ceiling and the floor shook underneath him with tremendous force, knocking him off his feet.

"Blimey!" Mortain exclaimed. "What?" Slowly, he calmed his breathing. Crinkling his brow, he determined there was only one way he would have been able to hear his name called within his mind.

Exactly then the loud creaking once again echoed across the room. He watched intently as the two tall wooden doors opened up to a pathway of complete darkness. Then, all became silent.

"Lord Kaeto?" Mortain uttered.

"Step inside," he heard the dragon say in his mind.

Mortain swallowed hard. "All right," he whispered, walking toward the doors. He turned back to look at his parents, smiling slightly.

"Make us proud, Son," Gearoid said, now standing beside his wife.

"I will. I promise," Mortain said, though he was feeling uncertain of his ability.

Please believe in me, he requested in his mind.

Mortain turned back to the darkness, took in a deep breath, exhaled, and walked inside, nervously glancing over his shoulder when he heard the doors close behind him.

CHAPTER TWO

DRACONIERA MOUNTAIN—
THE KINGDOM OF ARACELLY
1220 CE

"I can do this," Mortain whispered to himself. "I made a promise to Mum and Dad to make them proud. I must do this. I shall!" A misty fog filled the pathway when Mortain left the doorway. There was water dripping from above and occasionally a large drop splashed on the pathway in front of him. In the distance, he could see a room, which radiated a faint glow. Entering the room, he found himself in a large, round cavern. Small doorways lined either side, and a rock pedestal stood in the centre.

Mortain gazed up at the source of the glow, which seemed to be coming from a recessed shelf on the rock wall face, and let out a loud scream, having been startled by the sudden appearance of the magnificent dragon. From his father's stories, he knew Lord Kaeto was a dragon, but he didn't expect the dragon to be so enormous and all-encompassing.

"Mortain McKinnon!" Lord Kaeto said, watching Mortain run behind the rock pedestal and cower behind it in fear. "I order you to calm yourself!" He raised his head and roared, shaking their surroundings.

Mortain stopped screaming. He surreptitiously gazed around the pedestal. "You're...you're," Mortain stuttered, "Lord Kaeto?"

"Yes," the dragon answered telepathically.

Mortain slowly stood on his feet before continuing. "I don't understand. Why can I hear you talking in my head? I thought only warlocks can do that?"

Lord Kaeto blew smoke out of his nostrils. "You are a resident of the kingdom of Aracelly; therefore, you have been gifted with the ability to understand me."

Mortain chuckled. "Blimey! Am I really talking to a dragon? That's new. Reckoned you would never call for me. I mean, you're supposed to already know my future, do you not?"

"My knowledge of your future is irrelevant. All witches and warlocks of this kingdom are equally eligible to participate in the Rite of Wands."

"So, that means you'll permit me to participate? I'll be able to earn my magical powers?" Mortain's heart warmed, his face beginning to display hope. "Sorry. It's merely, my Mum, she always said I would not amount to anything."

Lord Kaeto studied him before answering. "Mortain McKinnon. You have been chosen to participate in the Rite of Wands ceremony in which your soul shall face the ultimate analysis. You will be taken on a journey of your lifetime, viewing portions of your past, present, and future. Do you accede?"

"Yes," Mortain answered, crinkling his brow. He could feel his heart start to race from a mix of anticipation and fear growing inside him.

"Then it shall begin! You may feel a tingling sensation as I investigate your essence," Lord Kaeto said. "Dragomir, come forward!"

Abruptly, there was a sound of a bolt sliding open and a loud creak came from the door located on the right side of the room. Out stepped what looked to be a teenage warlock wearing tall black boots, a black tunic with a golden lacing, royal blue breeches and a long-sleeved white linen shirt. His face was hidden behind an orange-and-golden mask shaped like a dragon's head. Once he had finished approaching, he bowed, at the waist, to Lord Kaeto.

"Mortain, this is Dragomir, my apprentice. He will be assisting me with the ritual," Lord Kaeto said, turning to his assistant. "Dragomir, you may rise. You may cast the spell announcing the commencing of the ritual, wand at the ready."

The warlock rose. Then he raised his right hand into the air and shouted, *"Forina olivet!"*

A lightning bolt crashed down beside Mortain, followed by the sound of drums beating. The sound gradually became louder until it matched every thump of Mortain's frantic heart.

"What's happening?" Mortain whimpered. "The air feels thicker. I…I feel so lightheaded. It's so hard to breathe."

The dragon turned back to Mortain. "Mortain. It is important to keep your eyes upon mine at all times. Do you understand?"

"Yes," Mortain whispered as his world was beginning to spin. The golden yellow colour of the dragon's eyes seemed to swirl around the room.

On Lord Kaeto's cue, Dragomir raised his wand again, this time pointing it straight at Mortain's chest.

However, before Dragomir was successfully able to cast *Gañoth*, the spell that signalled the beginning of the Rite of Wands ceremony, Mortain's eyes rolled into the back of his head and his knees buckled as the darkness engulfed him.

Confused, Dragomir examined his wand for any logical explanation of what had simply occurred. Unable to determine why, he looked back over to Lord Kaeto. "A thousand apologies, my lord. I'm afraid the participant lost consciousness before I was able to cast the spell."

"Very well. Loss of consciousness is necessary for the ceremony to commence," the dragon answered telepathically, closing his eyes. "Cast the spell and I shall access the young warlock's soul."

THE KINGDOM OF ARACELLY
1215 CE

WHERE AM I?

When Mortain next became aware of his surroundings, he was standing in a pew located in the back of a Catholic church. The organist was playing a rendition of "All Glory, Laud and Honour." Beside him, his parents did not take any notice of his presence. At the front of the church, off to the side of the alter, a group of young boys was leading the hymn. One of the boys was clearly distracted as he fumbled around with his loose parchments, trying his best to keep up.

Odd. That shorter boy in the middle looks exactly like me!

For a brief moment, they locked eyes with each other before the boy dropped his parchments. The music abruptly stopped.

Winifred turned to her husband and muttered under her breath, "Oh, here we go again. I cannot believe this embarrassment."

"Young Master McKinnon!" the vicar scolded, bringing down his staff and hitting the scroll lying on the podium. "Pay attention!"

Blimey! That IS me! I remember this! I was so nervous having Mum and Dad watching me during rehearsal. I only wanted to make them proud, but I only ever disappointed Mum.

"Yes, Father Peadar, I'm so sorry," the boy answered, his face beet red as he reached down for the parchments.

Winifred huffed. "So much like his father."

I wish Mum would stop.

The vicar turned back to the organist. "Again, from the beginning."

As the music started again, Gearoid leaned in and spoke to his wife with a warning tone. "Quit making a spectacle of yourself in the house of the Lord, woman, and be quiet," Gearoid hissed, affirming his position as head of the household.

She huffed again. "I shall not possibly be able to show my face in town for the rest of the week."

"All the better, my dear," Gearoid answered as the scene went dark.

DRACONIERA MOUNTAIN—
THE KINGDOM OF ARACELLY
1220 CE

WHEN THE scene disappeared, Mortain found himself back in Draconiera Mountain only moments before his Rite of Wands ceremony.

Mortain watched himself take in a deep breath, exhale, and walk inside the doors.

What? How did I get back here?

As soon as the doors were closed, Mortain noticed his Mum stand up and point toward the doors. "There, you see?"

"Winifred, please," Gearoid said, rubbing his hands through his hair. "Not now."

"I told you forcing the boy to participate now was a foolish idea. One look at him and you can clearly see he is not ready."

No, Mum. I am ready.

"Why do you doubt Mortain's capabilities? I did not force him. It is his right and he is no less prepared for his ceremony than I was at his age. Certainly, you were not prepared for the challenges you faced in yours, correct? Have a little faith. I'm confident he will succeed."

Listen to him, Mum. I can do this.

"Is that so? Honestly, Gearoid, it amazes me you have the accomplishments you have," Winifred said.

"I fail to see how any of this is relevant," Gearoid interrupted. "Mortain will pass his Rite of Wands ceremony and shall walk through those doors as a warlock from the kingdom of Aracelly. Even if he should not, he shall receive the best education possible."

Winifred huffed. "And I suppose that best education will come from you? Honestly, I dread the day you accept him for an apprenticeship."

What? Mum, what are you saying?

"Winifred be fair. There is no one better suited to teach him the path of a physician than his own father."

"My father disagrees. In fact, he has already provided me a list of recommendations for a Master."

"You would permit your father to deny my wishes? Mortain is *my* son! Not his."

"And he is his grandfather," Winifred retorted. "I'll tell you what you've suited Mortain for, Gearoid. A coward, that's what. Mortain has no idea of what he's up against. Blimey! I should have listened. My father was right. You've always been too easy on him. I'll promise you this, Gearoid. When Mortain fails his ceremony, my family shall forever hold you responsible for this atrocity."

Tears rolled down Mortain's face. Mum. *Why would you say these things about me? Do you not love me? Is my becoming a warlock the only thing that will earn me your love?* He clenched his fists. *I promise you, Mum. I will become a warlock. I will make the family proud. I shall keep our family's reputation and become a member of the magical community who is more powerful than you can ever imagine!*

Then all went dark.

MCKINNON ESTATE—
GLENDALOW
1260 CE

AGAIN, THE scene changed. At first, there was nothing but darkness. Slowly a magnificent estate was unveiled.

"Welcome home, Monsieur McKinnon," Armand announced, opening the door to the McKinnon estate.

"Thank you, Armand. It is good to be home," the elder McKinnon replied, unfastening his overcoat and handing it to Armand. "What news?"

Hang on. Is that me? This must be from my future! And, wait, I'm old. I'm very old. Older than my father, in fact! Blimey! When did I get to be so old?

"A pigeon delivered this letter. I believe it's of importance," Armand said, retrieving it and handing the rolled-up parchment over to Mortain.

"Thank you, Armand," Mortain answered.

"Is there anything else I can get for you, Monsieur McKinnon?" Armand asked as he watched Mortain unravel the parchment and walk toward his office.

An odour from a previous fire lingered on the parchment, but it didn't drown out the smell of death. Mortain didn't respond as he was already reading the missive. From his position as onlooker, young Mortain read too.

To my good friend Mortain McKinnon,

I write to you tonight with urgency. It is selfish of me to ask more of you after you freed me of my burden with Verlyn. I continue to feel his evil and believe it contributed to the death of your dear wife. I am glad that his existence has not caused you further harm. I wish I could report the same for me.

A plague has ravaged Edesia. I, along with other members of the church and physicians, have taken on the task to assist the ill. We have done what is necessary to protect ourselves; however, many have become ill themselves. People are dying in the hundreds, and the time to bury the dead properly alludes us. We are lost. I reckon in my heart this plague was brought down upon us as punishment from God due to my failure to rid the world of Verlyn.

Please. Your skill is desperately needed. I have complete faith you can stop what is killing us. I fear what may happen if you do not honour this request. I beg of you, burn this parchment after you have read it to prevent spread of the disease.

Your true loving,
Tiberius O'Brien

"Monsieur McKinnon?"

"Pardon?" the old man asked. Young Mortain could tell he was distracted by his own thoughts as he tried to comprehend the distraught words on the parchment. "Oh! Why, yes, there is something else you can do." He half laughed with embarrassment after collecting his thoughts. He cleared his throat. "Armand, would you please fetch Mierta for me? I need to speak with him about a rather, um, urgent matter."

Mierta? Who's that? Mortain asked himself.

"Oui, Monsieur McKinnon. Right away!"

Once Armand had left the room, Mortain placed the parchment down in a dish on his desk and set fire to it. He sighed heavily. Speaking to the air, he said solemnly, "So, the final events from my Rite of Wands have come, have they not? I suppose there really was no chance of altering my fate."

What? What am I going on about? What events? Mortain continued to watch himself as an adult.

"Father? Armand said you wished to see me."

Startled from his thoughts, Mortain turned to see Mierta standing in the doorway. His brow furrowed. Young Mortain felt a surge of recognition, even though he was sure he had never seen this person before.

"Ah, Mierta, my son!" Mortain smiled, standing from his desk chair, trying his best to hide his worry.

Mierta? I have a son? Blimey!

"Yes. I have received an urgent message from one of my mates residing in Edesia. A dreadful illness has reached their borders and my skill has been requested."

"I don't understand," Mierta said. "What would Edesia have need for the court physician representing the kingdom of Vandolay? Certainly, they have their own apothecaries to sort it out?"

I'm a court physician for a kingdom! Blimey! You'll see, Mum. I'll become a court physician. I'll join the Guild and study medicine in Poveglia. I'll become the greatest court physician ever known!

"Yes, that is true, but I suppose this illness may be beyond their skill. I reckon it is something I have encountered before; therefore, I can be of assistance. I can't imagine any other reason. Now, I must make my way without delay to Vandolay for an audience with His Majesty."

"Can't it wait till morning? You won't be any use to anyone if you haven't had proper sleep," Mierta said.

"You're right, my son. I apologise. I wish I could explain more at this time. I do not know when exactly I shall return. Therefore, Armand shall be informed you are head of house in my absence."

"But, Father! I must insist you rest first. I can ask Armand to get you a meal."

"Now, now, Mierta, no need to bother. Simply go on about your own business with those concoctions you have been occupying your time with. Though, when I shall return, I'll want to discuss why you appear to be quite bothered by them lately."

Mierta crinkled his brow. "Now I'll be the one to say not to bother. There's been a problem, yes, but I'll sort it out."

Mortain smiled. "And in that, my son, I'm confident you will. You are a McKinnon, and McKinnon's never give up no matter how grim the circumstances might be, you understand?"

"Yes, Father," Mierta answered, uncertain.

Mierta. That's a good name, Mortain thought, smiling, as the scene began to fade. *I must remember it for my future.*

CHAPTER THREE

DRACONIERA MOUNTAIN—
THE KINGDOM OF ARACELLY
1260 CE

Mortain gasped, quickly opening his eyes as he sat up. He looked around at his surroundings in a daze, not recalling how he got there.

"Ooh, blimey!" He groaned, reaching up for the back of his head, feeling pain pulsating from the beginnings of a medium-sized bump, barely registering that his hair seemed longer and thinner than it should have been. "Ouch! What?"

"I'm pleased to see you have decided to come back around, Master warlock," Lord Kaeto said, startling Mortain. "It is not common for my participants to lose consciousness without Dragomir's assistance."

"Lord Kaeto," Mortain uttered, quickly recalling what he had merely experienced. Without giving much thought to it, he stood up and bowed, in order to show his respect. "I apologise for screaming in your face. I should not have done that."

"Your apology has been accepted, though it is not necessary, nor is your bowing to me required."

"Mum believes I'm a coward," Mortain said to the floor before looking up at the dragon. "But I don't mean to be. I only want to be brave."

Lord Kaeto nodded. "And brave you must be, for what I am about to reveal shall not be easy to accept. Please, rise."

Confused, Mortain did as commanded, though he felt his legs shake underneath him and his bladder start to protest.

"Mortain McKinnon, the time has now come for you to accept your fate and complete the final stages of your life."

"Complete? What do you mean? I successfully completed my Rite of Wands, right? I can show Mum that she was wrong about me being cursed to a life as a Magulia, and I will be able to join the magical community, right?"

Lord Kaeto did not answer. Instead he merely gazed into Mortain's face.

Mortain's eyes filled with tears. There was a look in the dragon's golden eyes, which frightened him. He couldn't have failed, could he?

"I'm correct, am I not?" Mortain stammered. "I couldn't have failed my ceremony. I didn't…"

"No, you are correct. You did not fail your Rite of Wands ceremony. You were successfully evaluated, and your essence synced with the wand that will guide you throughout the rest of your life's journey."

Mortain crinkled his brows. "Then, what's wrong? Why do I feel like there's something important I'm missing? Have I done something to offend you?"

Lord Kaeto sighed deeply, realising Mortain actually believed he was experiencing his Rite of Wands for the very first time. "It would appear it is necessary to elaborate in order for you to remember."

"Remember? Remember what? My Rite of Wands? I remember it all! Mum not believing in me, convinced that I would bring shame to the family name, and then, there's Mierta. I'm going to have a son.

He's going to do extraordinary things and make me so proud!" Mortain said, his heart warming.

"Yes. That is all true. Mierta has a future that's special. Exactly like yours once was."

Mortain's heart began to race. "Once? I don't understand."

He turned to Dragomir without saying more. "Dragomir, I shall require your assistance once more. Would you retrieve the box containing the warlock's former wand? You recall where it has been contained all of these years, yes?"

Dragomir nodded. Without uttering any further words, he bowed and made his way back through the doors where he had first appeared.

Mortain laughed nervously. "Hang on. You said former. I haven't received my wand yet. You make it sound like I've endured the Rite of Wands before, but that's impossible."

"Is it now?" Lord Kaeto said. "Perhaps this will help unravel your mind. You did succeed in completing your Rite of Wands ritual. And you were given permission to practice spells and create concoctions. You were even given a wand to help you thrive in mastering the realm of healing magic. However, that was a long time ago."

Mortain's eyes widened with suspicion. "How long?"

"Nearly forty years ago."

"Forty? No, you're wrong. You're lying. If that were true, I would remember it! Like being a court physician! That was in my future in my Rite of Wands! I became a court physician. But in order to do so I must study medicine in Poveglia. Father told me only the brightest go there. That's where he studied!"

"That is correct," Lord Kaeto answered. "You did become one and were awarded an apprenticeship with one of my best healers. You became one of the finest court physicians in the history of the kingdom to serve Glendalow and Vandolay."

"Why do you keep referring to me in the past tense? It is annoying. That all happens in my future!"

"Happened," Lord Kaeto corrected. "Your memory is clouded in its process of beginning to shut down. That is to be expected for someone whose body experienced as ghastly a death as yours. Your spirit decided to return to one of the most important events of your life."

Mortain shook his head. "What are you going on about? That cannot be possible. I'm not dead. I'm right…"

His breath was abruptly cut off when he noticed Dragomir had returned through the opposite door. In his hands was a medium-sized brown wooden wand box held shut by two chains. Whatever was inside the box was desperately trying to get out.

Lord Kaeto lifted his mighty head and bellowed, "Behold what happens to a wand after a witch or warlock is punished through the Rite of Abnegation!"

"No!" Mortain cried, sinking to the ground, hearing his wand crying as if it was being tortured. He covered his ears with his hands. "Stop it! It wasn't my fault. It was an accident."

"An accident which you instigated, resulting in the death of your Master during your apprenticeship in Poveglia. As you will recall, it was decided through a trial you were to be stripped of your magic and to live the rest of your life as…" Lord Kaeto said.

"No!" Mortain interrupted, lowering his hands, recalling the events that led to his Rite of Abnegation. "I'm a warlock! I'm not a Magulia! I'm a warlock! I'm not a Magulia!"

His retort quieted when he began to hear what sounded like weeping in the distance.

"What's that? Where is it coming from? It sounds like someone's crying."

"That," Lord Kaeto began, "is your son crying."

"Mierta?" Mortain said, confused. "Why? I don't understand."

"He has discovered your dead body on the bedroom floor."

"No." Mortain shook his head as he looked down. He no longer saw himself as a twelve-year-old; instead, he was an old man. The front of his long white nightshirt was covered in blood, appearing as if he had violently vomited over it. "This cannot be happening!"

"I'm afraid it is so. He has failed to save you. Observe!" He turned, nodding his head at Dragomir.

The warlock raised his wand and chanted, "*Wapakoneta!*"

Heavy mist appeared before them, as if water was shimmering from ceiling to floor. A picture began to form in the mist until it resonated an image of Mierta.

He had walked into his father's bedroom at the McKinnon estate. They watched as Mierta lowered to his knees and moved a hand to his mouth, arranging it into a fist, before preparing himself for the worst. He placed a finger over Mortain's neck, confirming his father was dead. Mierta bowed his head and began to cry while laying a hand over his father's shoulder.

"No," Mortain whispered, tears forming in his own eyes. He once again saw the same white nightshirt still covered in blood.

"I'm sorry," Mierta whispered, tears rolling down his cheeks. "I'm sorry I failed you."

"No, you didn't fail me," Mortain cried. "Mierta, listen to me! It's the Shreya. The Shreya is coming to Iverna! You must find a way to stop it before it kills us all!" He stopped yelling to Mierta, abruptly coming to the realisation he would not have known that information if he was still experiencing his Rite of Wands ceremony.

"He cannot hear you," Lord Kaeto responded. "It is futile."

"It's true, then. I'm dead. I'm really dead," Mortain said, his eyes widening as he stared back at the dragon. Slowly, he placed his hand over the centre of his chest, realising he could no longer feel his heart beating.

"Indeed, in the last moments of your life, you are reliving your most important memories, especially your Rite of Wands. You have returned to the same place of your ceremony because it is my duty to help your soul pass over; however, before I do that, there is one more thing for you to know. You have succeeded in doing your part.

While you may have failed in stopping the Shreya, this story was never meant to be yours. Rather, this story belongs to your son and one other warlock whose life path has already been forced to cross with Mierta's. Together, they shall determine the fate of this land."

TWELVE
YEARS
EARLIER

CHAPTER FOUR

DRACONIERA MOUNTAIN—
THE KINGDOM OF ARACELLY
1248 CE

"Why is it so hot in here? I feel like I could faint!" Lochlann said, his frustrated tone echoing against the rough rock walls inside the mountain. He wiped the sweat from his brow with the sleeve of his black-and-red robe.

Mierta sighed and rolled his eyes, having heard enough of his younger brother's complaining.

"Lochlann," he said, brushing his brown bangs out of his green eyes, positioning them toward the right side of his face, "you do realise Draconiera Mountain is sitting over a hot spring, right? It's going to be sizzling! Now, quit your squawking and follow me."

He reached into the pocket of his breeches, pulling out a wand made of Gabon ebony with a bloodstone crystal positioned at the shaft. He held the wand in front of him.

"*Scamos lias!*" Mierta chanted, lighting the path before them, revealing ginger stonework.

Mierta shook his head as he continued forward. *I should have expected him not to know that. Even though he can be rather daft I must remind myself to be patient with him. After all, Lochlann didn't inherit Mother or Father's intelligence like I did.*

When Mierta noticed Lochlann had hesitated from proceeding further, he turned to face him.

"Come along, Lochlann. Keep up! The Rite of Wands won't be waiting for you all day."

Mierta remembered how his father had tried to encourage him on the day of his own Rite of Wands ten years ago. Mierta recalled how harrowing it had been for him to endure. It was a shame their father had decided not to attend Lochlann's, but Mortain felt Mierta was better suited because he was a warlock.

Mierta was anxious for his brother but knew the ritual was the initiation into the magical community, and it was the only way Lochlann would be allowed to make potions and cast spells. He reminded himself that he should be reassuring Lochlann, but he had difficulty controlling his impatience.

Lochlann let out a deep breath, nodding before continuing.

Mierta led him through a winding path toward the area where other anxious witches and warlocks were waiting their turn to experience their Rite of Wands ceremony. He observed Draconiera Mountain hadn't changed since he had successfully endured his own ritual. He still felt the sweltering air he was forced to inhale into his lungs, the sound of bubbling water from below filling his ears, and the dense fog attempting to compromise his vision.

"Mierta," Lochlann said nervously, interrupting his brother's thoughts, "why couldn't Father have been here? It's not fair; he was there for you."

"I don't know." Mierta shrugged, staring at the ground momentarily. "This kind of thing makes him uncomfortable. Perhaps because

Mum was a witch and he, a man. Trust me, it is best he is not here. He can't possibly comprehend what a warlock must go through since he's never experienced it himself; whereas, I can."

"Mierta…wait," Lochlann spoke anxiously.

Mierta stopped, slightly hesitating before turning around. He glanced back at Lochlann with concern.

Lochlann shook his head. "I don't think I can do this. I'm going to fail!"

"Hey," Mierta said, approaching him. "It's all right. Calm yourself and take a few slow breaths," he instructed, leaning toward his brother with a smile. Crinkling his brow, he squatted so they were eye to eye. He studied Lochlann carefully, trying to determine the right words to say. It amazed him sometimes how different he and Lochlann were and yet at this precise moment, so alike. He gently placed his hands over his brother's shoulders. "Listen," he said in a soft voice, "you don't have to go through the ceremony if you don't wish to. Before the ceremony starts, Lord Kaeto will ask you to accede. All you have to do is say no. Then, it will be over, and we can start the return journey home."

"But then I'll only be a man," Lochlann replied.

"Yes, but," Mierta said, carefully selecting his words, "choosing to be a man is nothing to be ashamed of. Our father, for example, is a court physician, and the majority of the residents living in Glendalow and Vandolay are not witches or warlocks either! Whatever you decide, you will make Mum and Dad proud."

"You think so?" Lochlann asked.

"I know so." Mierta smiled.

"But Mum is dead," Lochlann retorted. "She never even got the chance to really know me. How would you know how she feels?"

"That's not the point," Mierta interrupted. "The point is—" He stopped speaking mid-sentence, realising the conversation needed to shift toward a different direction. "The point is if you should change your mind, you'll need to be brave. Remember this: the Rite of Wands is not simply a test—it has driven witches and warlocks to madness."

At that very moment a witch holding her hands to her ears crashed into Mierta.

"Pardon, can I help you?" Mierta asked.

The witch's eyes looked far away and incoherent. Instead of responding with words, a bloodcurdling scream erupted from her mouth. She blindly took off running again into the darkness. Mierta was unconcerned as he assumed her parents would be soon following to care for her.

Frightened, Lochlann breathed a couple quick breaths in and out. "Blimey! What do you reckon is wrong with her?"

"She didn't pass," Mierta answered matter-of-factly, though he felt shaken by the undesirable encounter. Mierta tightened his grip on his brother's shoulders, a sound of urgency to his voice. "Lochlann, it is now more important than ever for you to understand how the Rite of Wands ceremony works. It will determine your fate and whether you will become part of the magical community, or if you should be forced to live the remainder of your life as a Magulia, a person unable to perform magic. Now hurry up! We will be late for sure," Mierta said, striding toward the waiting area.

"I don't care about being able to perform magic," Lochlann blurted, watching his brother walk away. "I only want to be like you, and I want you to be proud of me, big brother!"

Mierta's eyes widened as he furrowed his eyebrows. Prior to this very moment, it had not occurred to him that Lochlann's future may turn out to be as grim as his. Having seen his own death in his Rite of Wands, he could not fathom Lochlann being unscathed if he saw something similar. He had been so preoccupied with his own challenges that he had completely neglected that possibility.

Mierta shook out the light from his wand and placed it back in the pocket underneath his robe. As he approached closer, he squatted to Lochlann's height. Observing how oily his brother's shoulder-length black hair was, he gently brushed it back out of Lochlann's brown eyes. He stared into his face, letting out a long, deep breath before providing him with a small smile.

"Then," he began before becoming serious again, "no matter what happens, you must succeed and become a warlock." He then stood up and began to walk away again. "That is the only way you'll ever be like me." Mierta frowned. *I should have told Lochlann everything that will happen in the ceremony even though it is forbidden. There is no way Lochlann will pass. My reputation will be ruined! Lochlann is way too thick. Even if by some miracle he passes, he'll never manage to be like me!* Mierta couldn't resist letting his arrogant thoughts slip through sometimes.

Mierta retrieved his wand from his robe once more and lit their way as they continued walking in silence, eventually reaching the anteroom.

Lochlann looked around at the others waiting their turn. He noticed that most of them looked as scared as he felt.

Mierta, in the meantime, started looking around for a place to prepare to sit and wait.

"Mierta? Will it hurt?"

"What?" Mierta said, keeping his back toward his brother.

"The Rite of Wands. Will it hurt?" Lochlann asked.

"Yes," Mierta answered, his voice giving away a small teasing smile. He turned around. "Are you afraid of pain? What happened to that brave knight who once stabbed me with a wooden sword to rescue the queen?" Mierta said playfully, trying to lighten his little brother's mood.

Lochlann's eyes grew wide; he wasn't so easily distracted. He swallowed hard and expelled air through his mouth.

"You can't expect it to be easy, now can you?" Mierta teased, taking a seat. "Now, this is when things get really exciting!"

"What do you mean?" Lochlann inquired, taking a seat next to his brother.

"Blimey, Lochlann, you really are that daft, aren't you?" Mierta said, shaking his head. He pointed. "See those two tall wooden doors? That is the entrance to the Rite of Wands. In a moment we shall get to see a witch or warlock walk through them, either as a full-fledged member of our magical community or as a Mag…"

His sentence was abruptly cut short by a sound he was very familiar with. A loud creaking echoed across the room, shaking the ground underneath their feet, as the two tall wooden doors opened to a pathway of complete darkness.

Everyone waited, staring silently, wondering when the candidate would appear through the doors. All of a sudden, screams filled the anteroom.

Quickly, Mierta removed his wand from his robe. Though protecting other people by magic wasn't his nature, he wasn't about to allow anything to harm his younger brother. Positioning his wand at the ready, he noticed several young witches and warlocks were panicking over the sight of a large brown rat with a golden radiance around it skittering out between the doors.

"I don't believe it," Mierta uttered before a loud puff of smoke engulfed the rat. He watched intently until the smoke faded, revealing a beautiful witch kneeling with one knee bent, holding up a wand made of maple with a charoite crystal infused at the shaft. Applause filled the room.

"Who's that?" Lochlann asked, perplexed.

"Master Ezekiel's daughter," Mierta answered, rolling his eyes. "Her name's Zorina. She is the only witch that has been able to master therianthrope prior to going through the Rite of Wands, allowing her to physically transform into any animal of her choice. Reckon I met her the first day of my apprenticeship. She, as a cat, had hidden herself on the top of one of the bookshelves in the back of the shop. She's actually your age, but due to accidentally drinking one of her father's concoctions, she's now permanently trapped in the body and mind of a twenty-four-year-old woman."

"That's brilliant." Lochlann laughed, becoming smitten by Zorina's beautiful appearance.

"Nonsense! There's nothing brilliant about it at all," Mierta answered. "Trust me. She simply likes to get attention. Honestly, I'm surprised she didn't decide on taking the appearance of a bird instead of a rat, considering how much she loves to fly."

"Lochlann McKinnon."

Lochlann gasped, realising he was the only one who heard his name announced telepathically.

Hearing his brother's gasp, Mierta turned. "What is it?" He could see fear in Lochlann's eyes.

Lochlann's voice broke as he whispered in a higher-pitched tone. "Reckon I'm going mad. I heard my name being called in my mind!"

Mierta laughed, taking control of the situation. He clapped his hands together and snapped his fingers. "Lochlann, you are not going mad. That was Lord Kaeto. Your time to participate in the Rite of Wands has come. Go on, then," Mierta encouraged. "I will be waiting for you right here. I promise. Remember to be brave and make Mum and Dad proud."

"Step inside, Lochlann McKinnon," Lochlann heard the dragon say.

"I don't know if I can do this," Lochlann said before expelling the air from his lungs. He clenched his fists before proceeding forward into the darkness.

Mierta watched until the doors closed behind his brother. "Good luck," he whispered under his breath. "You'll need it."

× ✕ ×

MIERTA TURNED, his brow crinkling, when he heard the familiar sound of the two wooden doors opening.

The room went silent as the anticipation grew. Not even a pin drop could be heard as everyone turned their attention to the dark pathway. It felt like an eternity before the sound of footsteps was heard, and slowly, Lochlann stepped from the darkness.

"Lochlann?" Mierta questioned, concerned, observing his younger brother's flushed face and the staggering in his walk. "You all right?"

Lochlann attempted to speak, but all that came out of his mouth were words that were incomprehensible.

No, no, no! Mierta's thoughts raced, fearing his brother had failed the ceremony. He quickly approached him.

"You're trembling. What happened? Did you see something wrong with your future?" Mierta said, his eyes rapidly moving side to side, studying Lochlann's face for any other signs of madness.

Before he permitted Lochlann a chance to answer, Mierta continued, "Your wand. Where is it? Show it to me."

"Mierta," Lochlann said, but before he could say more, his knees buckled.

"Lochlann?" Mierta said, catching his younger brother as he began to collapse in a dead faint. *What did you see?*

CHAPTER FIVE

ORLYND'S COTTAGE—
THE KINGDOM OF VANDOLAY
1248 CE

Orlynd had retreated to his own private cottage that the king had given him. The clank and clatter of the castle could be too much to bear, and he needed a quiet place to relax and prepare for the following day. He lay on his little cot and quickly fell asleep.

A few hours later, Orlynd startled awake to the sound of the ringing bells of Tower Chainnigh, which only rang when someone from the castle had died. Glancing around his bedroom, he observed the sun was starting to rise. Then, he heard the bells again.

"Whit? Nay. Nay. Nae again," he said, throwing the sheets from his body, nearly stumbling over his feet as he approached the closet for a change of attire. After pulling his robe on over his nightshirt, Orlynd ran out the door through the town and toward the castle grounds. He passed several carts and booths that were being made ready for the day's market. Fruits were being stacked on tables, meats were being hung on hooks, and vegetables fresh from the fields were being pulled out of bags.

As Orlynd approached the gate he was temporarily blocked by two guards. Once they recognised who he was, they let him pass. He continued forward until he spotted a gathering of people in the court-yard off to the left. Pushing himself, he made his way toward them, over the manicured lawns, skirting the shrubs and flowers. Orlynd took a few moments to gather his breath before entering the circle of people. He saw King Déor, Mortain McKinnon, the court physi-cian, and a guard named Aindrias looking down at a pile. He was shocked to realise that a guard, or rather what was left of one, lay on the ground in front of them.

"Orlynd," Déor said, acknowledging his presence.

"Yir Majesty," Orlynd whispered, bowing. "Whit happened here?"

Mortain cleared his throat. "Yes, well, we were merely discussing the attack from overnight, isn't that right?" he said.

"Aye. It's exactly like the other guard that was found floating in the horse trough last week," Aindrias said. "His face was beyond recognition. His tunic had been ripped to shreds, soaked in his blood, and his legs were bent at odd angles as if he had fallen from a great height."

"Based on my examination of the body, the guard appears to have been attacked by some sort of animal. Only, there are no animal tracks to confirm those suspicions," Mortain said.

"Perhaps it was a wolf? Or an animal that can fly? Orlynd," Déor said, "have you overheard any commoners in the kingdom speaking of seeing such an animal?"

"Nay, Yir Majesty."

Déor nodded. "Everyone, keep your ears open. If you hear any-thing, anything that can give us an understanding into who or what is attacking my guards, report it to me or Queen Anya immediately."

"Yes, Your Grace," the group responded before breaking off in their own separate directions.

Orlynd hung back as the body was covered by Mortain and prepared to be removed. He could not help but think about what the king had said. It could have been a wolf attack, but something didn't add up. The scratches and gouges in the body looked to have been made by talons of some sort, very large talons to be sure. However, Orlynd could not think of any bird that was that large. It would require him to do some additional research.

"Yir Majesty, Ah request access tae yir ancient scrolls wit yir permission," Orlynd said.

"Yes, of course, granted, but may I inquire why?" Déor answered.

"Reckon thir may be a clue tae identifying whit is attacking the guards. Ah suspect thir may be an additional force at play."

"Another force? Explain."

"Ah cannae yet, Yir Majesty, but it is possible it may nae be a natural creature."

"I see," Déor replied. "Very well. You'll find them inside Tower Chainnigh. Seek out Beatrice Calderon. She is the keeper of scrolls. I will write a note to her allowing you access to them."

"Aye, Ah know Lady Calderon. We huv met before."

Déor glanced over at Orlynd, surprised. "You have?"

"Aye," Orlynd answered, observing the troubled look on the king's face. "Dinnae worry yirself, Yir Majesty. Ah met her when Ah goat lost during ma first week here."

"Mmm," Déor said, wondering if there was more to Orlynd's story or not. He had been unaware that Beatrice and Orlynd had met.

"Right, then. Ah'll take ma leave."

DRACONIERA MOUNTAIN—
THE KINGDOM OF ARACELLY
1248 CE

"LOCHLANN," MIERTA spoke, slowly lowering himself to the ground as he carefully laid his brother's body down. He studied his brother with concern, observing the steady rise and fall of his chest and the stammering of his heart through the vein in his neck.

The Rite of Wands can be very frightening, but I never truly thought Lochlann might actually fail his ceremony!

Mierta crinkled his brow, recalling how his own Rite of Wands had been a harrowing experience. Absentmindedly, he reached up to touch the scar on the left side of his face. The burn and sting from the injury had long passed; however, the consequences of his actions would remain a constant reminder to him.

He turned, realising everyone was staring at them. "Bugger off, you lot! Give him some space!"

"Will he be all right, sir?" a young witch asked.

"Pardon?" Mierta said, searching for who asked the question. His eyes came upon a petite witch wearing an emerald-coloured robe. Her frizzy blonde hair looked like a spell had gone wrong. "Yes, yes, he simply lost consciousness."

"Is that what happens when you become a Magulia?" she asked.

"What?" Mierta froze when he heard the girl's question. He answered as if he had been insulted. "No! No!"

He switched his attention to Lochlann.

"Come on, Lochlann, wake up," Mierta scolded, trying his best to convince himself Lochlann was merely playing games for attention as he lightly smacked the sides of his brother's cheeks.

"How do you know?" she questioned, watching Mierta remove a satchel from around his cape and begin to sort through it.

Mierta paused, crinkling his brow. He looked up at her before turning his gaze back toward the satchel. "I don't."

"Then, he really could be one, could he not?" she challenged.

"No," Mierta answered. "I refuse to accept that. I'll not have my brother be looked upon as an outcast. Aha! Knew I had it in here somewhere." He pulled out a small flask from his satchel. He grinned, pleased.

"What are you doing?" she asked, watching Mierta unscrew the top.

"What does it look like I'm doing?" Mierta answered quickly, placing a portion of the flask under Lochlann's nose, allowing the aroma and a white, smoky powder to fill his nostrils. "Waking him up!"

Exactly then, Lochlann awoke and sat straight up. "Blimey, Mierta!" he said between a series of coughs. "What did you put in that. One-month-old horse manure?"

"I'm relieved your sense of humour is still intact," Mierta said, closing the flask. "That was sal ammoniac."

"Sala what?" Lochlann gagged, covering his mouth with his hands to keep himself from vomiting.

"Sal ammoniac. It's a mineral composed of ammonium chloride and—oh, never mind. Why do I even bother?" Mierta said, noticing what appeared to be a wand hanging out from the side of Lochlann's robe. He quickly reached and grabbed the wand, revealing it. A large gasp from the group of young witches and warlocks could be heard as he pointed it toward them, swinging it side to side.

"Ha! There. See? Wand. He's not a Magulia," Mierta said, satisfied.

"Give me that," Lochlann said, reaching for his wand.

Instead, Mierta turned, shielding it from his brother. "Not until you prove to me your mind is still intact. Call for your wand."

"I can't," Lochlann said.

Mierta laughed. "Oh, come on. Of course you can! You're a warlock. Reach out your hand and call for it like I do."

"I told you before, I can't."

Mierta laughed again. "Lochlann, I know your mind can be slow. Tell me, did you already forget the words for the spell? It's all right if you did. I can tell you."

"I'm never going to use magic!" Lochlann blurted out.

"Why?" Mierta asked, lowering Lochlann's wand. "You aren't a Magulia." He studied his brother's face. "No. You're afraid. But, why? Why would you be afraid to use it? You're part of the magical community now. You're a warlock. It's part of who you are." Mierta gestured around at the crowd. "Part of who *we* are."

"Let it go, Mierta," Lochlann said. He reached out for his wand. "You know I can't talk about my Rite of Wands ceremony. Now, please, give me back my wand. I want to go home."

Mierta crinkled his brow and eyed him suspiciously. "Fine," he said, handing back the wand. "But don't think this conversation is over. I'm going to find out what you're hiding."

TOWER CHAINNIGH—
THE KINGDOM OF VANDOLAY
1248 CE

"SCAMOS LIAS!"

Orlynd held out his hand and stared into the centre of a dark abyss of what seemed like an endless, winding stone staircase.

"Crickey," Orlynd muttered to himself, rubbing his hand through his beard. "Ah huv forgotten how far down this staircase wis."

The stairs were attached to the walls of the tower, the centre of which was open to the air. As he made his way down the stairs, he could see a faint light glowing from underneath a doorframe.

The door was made of a dark wood held together by hammered metal. There were designs of the same hammered metal shaped like various persons. Semi-circular shapes at the top and bottom half seemed to enclose the hinges. Along the bottom was a braided metal piece that stretched the width of the door. The iron door handle and hinges had darkened with age.

Once he had passed through the doorway, he again found himself inside a cavernous room filled with bookshelves that seemingly never ended. The tables and chairs were still stationed between the bookshelves, some of which were covered in papers and scrolls exactly as he remembered them to be. He delighted in seeing the sculpture of the known universe still standing in the very centre of the room.

"Orlynd O'Brien!" an older woman said while Orlynd was shaking the light out of his wand. "Is that you?"

"Aye," Orlynd said, putting his wand away. He turned to see the keeper of scrolls, Beatrice Calderon, wearing a heavily embroidered dress in dark brown tones with light blue accents. Her grey hair was hidden under a cloth crown that matched her dress, with a light brown veil flowing down over her shoulders.

"It has been ten years since you wandered down here. Why, if I recall correctly, the last time was the night of King Francis's passing. Uncertain you were about your role here then."

Orlynd nodded, feeling a bit guilty. It was normal for residents of the kingdom to visit the library, either to read, research, or have a think. However, since King Francis's passing, Orlynd hadn't given himself permission to return until now, on official business, fearful that he would be looked upon as a bad omen because of what happened last time he was here.

"You have nothing to fear. I can see the troubled expression on your face. Please, tell me what is bothering you."

Orlynd cleared his throat and handed her the note from the king. "Ah'm in need oaf a scroll oan the creatures found in this kingdom. Specifically…eh…monsters. But, Ah dinnae know where tae search!"

"Monsters you say?" Beatrice said, a bit perplexed.

"Aye. There's been an animal who has been attacking n killing members oaf the king's guard. No oan has seen it tae be able tae provide a proper description, but Ah reckon it is very large n has oversized talons."

"I see." Beatrice thought for a moment. "No creature can I recall hearing of as you describe in our kingdom. However—"

"Something dinnae feel right," Orlynd interrupted. "Ah dinnae understand. It's like there may huv been an additional force at play here. Ah fear someone may huv used magic tae conjure this creature."

"A magical creature, you say?" she said, raising an eyebrow. "Hmm. Then, perhaps, may I suggest you start searching through the books found in the section on myths and legends? One of the books you may find there is a bestiary, an encyclopaedia full of illustrations and descriptions of all the animals found in our land. Now, where did I move them to? Did a bit of reorganising recently, and, well…" She trailed off, turning and walking down a long aisle.

Orlynd decided to follow.

"No, not there. That's the children's section." She stopped and looked around, a bit confused. "Maybe over there? No, that's where I keep all the books on ailments. I really should turn those over to the court physician. I keep forgetting." She turned down another long aisle filled with books and scrolls. "Ah, yes, here it is," she said, picking up one of the books from the shelf and handing it over to Orlynd. "*The Folklore of Iverna* by Ailionora Healy; she is a scholar from the kingdom of Aracelly. All the books she has written on Iverna's history can be found in this library. Her expertise, one would say, is in our land's history. If such a creature may exist, she would have documented it in this encyclopaedia. That I'm certain of."

Orlynd nodded his head and smiled, eager to start searching. "Thank yis!"

He raced over to the closest table and set the book down. Quickly, he flipped to the first page, finding himself entranced by a tale on the legendary mystical beings named the Aos Sí.

CHAPTER SIX

MCKINNON ESTATE—
GLENDALOW
1248 CE

Father!" Mierta called as he and Lochlann entered the McKinnon estate. He took off his royal blue robe, hung it over the coatrack, and did the same with Lochlann's.

Noticing his father hadn't answered his initial call, he turned and looked up in the direction of the stairway leading to the sleeping quarters. He shouted again, "Father? We've returned from Lochlann's Rite of Wands!"

Again, there was no answer.

That is odd. I wonder where he's gone off to? Mierta thought.

"Do you reckon Father is home?" Lochlann asked, also noticing their father hadn't acknowledged Mierta's calls.

"I don't know. He may be upstairs resting or may have been summoned to the kingdom of Vandolay again. Nonetheless, we can't be bothered," he said, smiling, smacking his hands together. "It's tea-time! A most perfect time to celebrate your induction into the magical community. We can tell Father all about it when he returns. I'll put the kettle on. Reckon Armand has probably already gotten a fresh pot. Go on now, into the parlour with you. I'll join you at the table shortly."

After watching Lochlann walk toward the parlour, Mierta turned and followed the wooden flooring until he bumped into Armand coming out of the kitchen, carrying a tray of biscuits and two cups of tea.

"Armand," Mierta said, observing the spilled tea on the tray and his servant's shirt. "I was unaware you were in here."

"So sorry, Monsieur. The fault is mine. I will retrieve a new tray and biscuits," Armand said. "Please, forgive me for not informing you Monsieur McKinnon is not here."

Armand, their family's servant, was a tall man a few years older than Mierta. His long, curly black hair had been tied back at the base of his neck. A short, well-trimmed beard covered his strong jawline, and his upper lip was covered by a thin moustache.

"Of course he isn't," Mierta said with a bit of annoyance. "Where'd he go off to this time?"

"A pigeon arrived with a letter summoning him to the kingdom of Vandolay."

Mierta sighed impatiently. "Ah. Yes, yes, I understand. Duty calls. Rather unfortunate though. I had wished to speak to him about something important that I wished to keep private. No matter. I'll handle it myself."

"Oui, Monsieur. I'll put the kettle back on and bring it out to the table when it's ready."

"Thank you, Armand."

Mierta watched Armand retreat to his quarters for a new change of clothing before putting the kettle back on the fire. Then his eyes fell upon Lochlann seated at the cherrywood table next to three matching, comfy chairs, turning his wand in his hand as if he were deep in thought about something.

Mierta's footsteps echoed on the wooden floor as he entered the parlour and approached the table, but Lochlann didn't look up. Mierta quickly retrieved his wand from his breeches pocket, pointed it at Lochlann's wand and shouted, "*Palavariso!*"

Lochlann's wand immediately flew out of his hand and landed on the other side of the room.

"Blimey, Mierta! Why did you go and do that for?" Lochlann cried.

"I told you before. I'm going to find out what you're hiding. Reach out your hand and call for your wand. Come on now, I know you can do it."

Lochlann sighed, frustrated. "Are you really that thick? I already told you back at Draconiera Mountain. I can't!"

"And I don't believe you," Mierta answered. He stared at Lochlann for a few minutes, watching him refuse to call for his wand. Mierta rolled his eyes. "Fine, then. I'll demonstrate."

He threw his own wand across the room, watching it land near Lochlann's.

"Have you gone mad?" Lochlann asked.

"I'm no madder than you are, Lochlann. In fact, I would almost accuse you of not being happy that you are a warlock."

"That's not the case."

"Isn't it?" Mierta said, unconvinced. "Prove it." He reached out his hand and concentrated, his eyes beginning to take on the appearance of snake eyes, before he chanted, "*Convosuri!*"

Lochlann watched as his brother's wand rose from the ground and flew into Mierta's hand. He placed it back into his breeches.

"Now, you do it."

Lochlann sighed with exasperation. "You're wasting your time, Mierta. You forget I don't possess your gift of telekinesis. Dragomir had to bring out my wand still in its box."

Mierta stopped momentarily as he thought it over, raising his index finger. "Right. Stay there." He walked over to retrieve Lochlann's wand from the floor before placing it in his brother's hand.

"Now," Mierta instructed, grabbing a hold of Lochlann's hand and guiding it in the direction of the fireplace. "Those logs of wood in there—I want you to light them on fire."

"What? But it's summertime," Lochlann complained.

"A little fire isn't going to hurt," Mierta said. "Just get on with it."

Lochlann sighed. "I don't know the spell."

Standing behind his brother, Mierta silently mimicked him. He then grabbed the bridge of his nose, rubbed his eyes and said, *"Sine."*

"Sine," Lochlann said, prompting the logs to burst into flame.

"Now, see? That wasn't difficult, was it?" Mierta said, smiling softly. He reached into his breeches for his wand, raised it toward the flames, and made a clockwise motion with his wand before commanding, *"Tíofria!"*

Promptly, the flames extinguished and were replaced by a layer of ice.

Lochlann rolled his eyes. "You don't understand," Lochlann said, setting his wand down on the table.

Mierta crinkled his brow. "Then, explain it to me so I *do* understand," he said, sitting down in the chair at the other end of the table.

"I can't," Lochlann answered.

"But, you can!" Mierta said, leaning in. "You can trust me. I want to help you."

Lochlann didn't answer or make eye contact with his brother.

Mierta's eyes rapidly looked Lochlann up and down as his mind attempted to sort things out. "You said you couldn't do magic. I proved to you now that you can do magic." He eyed Lochlann suspiciously. "Magic. That's it, isn't it? Lochlann, in your Rite of Wands, did you see yourself casting a spell in the future that does harm? Is that what's bothering you?"

Lochlann didn't answer.

THE RITE OF ABNEGATION

"Lochlann, listen to me. Your future can be changed," Mierta said, moving his hands like a conductor. "The Rite of Wands isn't fixed in stone. Trust me. You can hone your skills and avoid using whatever spell caused…"

"That's not what happened!" Lochlann interrupted, standing up from his chair.

"Then, what?"

"I can't tell you! I can't tell anyone!" Lochlann shouted. Then he took off for his bedroom.

"Lochlann," Mierta whispered, shock displayed over his face.

TOWER CHAINNIGH—
THE KINGDOM OF VANDOLAY
1248 CE

IT WAS now at least very late in the evening, maybe even the early hours of the next morning. The empty table, which he had first sat at, was now covered in various scrolls, books, and loose papers. Orlynd had honestly lost track of how long he had been searching for a picture or even some kind of description that matched the traces left behind by the unknown creature. He wasn't even sure if there was anyone left present in the library underneath Tower Chainnigh based on how quiet things had become. Perhaps he had even fallen asleep himself at one point, too?

"Still searching, you are?" Beatrice said, replacing one of the candles in the nearby candelabra whose flame had been extinguished some time ago.

Orlynd sat up, stretched and let out the sound of a big yawn. "Aye."

"No luck finding the creature, I take," Beatrice said.

"Nay." Orlynd sighed. "But, Ah believe ma father wid huv enjoyed these books. He loved tae read n thir r many stories definitely influenced by the church. Ah almost wid say eywis stories were all picked by them."

"Is that so?" Beatrice smiled.

Orlynd continued to ramble. "The illustrations r lovely. Ah especially enjoyed the stories about the Aos Sí. Did yis know thir's a bird called the caladrius? Its faeces can cure poor eyesight n its glance can determine if someone will die."

"Mmm. Why, yes. I believe I once encountered such a bird in King Francis's study. It had the misfortune of ending up as game during a celebration for the king one year. As I recall the king was not happy seeing his pet served up for supper."

"Oh," Orlynd sighed before returning to the original topic, "thir's nae any records ay any such creature thit Ah huv been able tae find. Ah'm starting tae fear ma searching has been fir naught."

He turned the page of the encyclopaedia and stared down at the page in front of him. There was a large illustration of a creature of legend, believed to have been conjured by druids. It had the head of a Krampus, a body of a lion, claws of an eagle, wings of a black bird, and the tail of a snake. Orlynd's blood ran cold.

"The Sulchyaes," he whispered, his eyes growing wide. *How did Ah miss this before?!*

Then, in the distance, they heard what sounded like an explosion. The library's structure gave a little shake, followed by the sound of multiple screams coming from above.

Orlynd stood up from his seat and turned to Beatrice.

"The castle is under attack!" Orlynd said, looking up toward the direction of the bells. He started to move away from the table and then stopped. He turned back to Beatrice. "Ah'm sorry fir leaving this mess, but Ah must find the king."

"There is no need to apologise. I understand," Beatrice answered, watching Orlynd nod his head with acknowledgement. "You'll find a hidden entrance to the castle connected to the servant's kitchen. Take the Bumbling Staircase and you'll gain quick access to the king's private apartments."

"Aye," Orlynd said, not mentioning that he was already familiar with the entrance, having had to use it the night King Francis passed.

She reached down and lifted *The Folklore of Iverna* by Ailionora Healy from the desk and handed it to Orlynd. "Take it. I believe this encyclopaedia will find better use with you than remaining down here. Now, go! Protect the king!" she said, watching Orlynd turn to make his leave. She folded her hands and bowed her head, saying a quick prayer.

COINNEACH CASTLE—
THE KINGDOM OF VANDOLAY
1248 CE

DÉOR AWOKE with a scream on his lips. It took him little more than a few seconds to realise it was the sound of something exploding followed by the piercing cry of an animal that had awoken him. He grabbed his robe as he jumped out of bed and hurried to the window.

Looking out he saw and heard chaos. Guards were running, seemingly, every which way. Some were shooting firebrand arrows into the air while others were attending to the injured where a barrel containing potassium nitrate had combusted.

The castle is under attack. Why did no one notify me? And where is my valet de chambre?

"Jakub!" he shouted. He stood near the edge of his bed and waited impatiently for his servant to appear and assist him into his attire.

After his servant failed to arrive, Déor rushed over to his armoire, opening it to find a fresh set of clothing the Master of Wardrobe had put inside the evening before. Quickly, he dressed in dark blue hose, a white cotton shirt with a drawstring tie at the neck, and a royal blue tunic. He fastened his leather belt at his waist and slipped on his knee-high leather boots. Fully attired, he took a hold of his family's sword, Ruairí, which was leaning against one of the tables near his bed, before releasing it from its sheath. He rushed to the door and opened it, prepared to defend his castle.

"Orlynd," Déor said with surprise, meeting him at the other side of the door. There were bags under the warlock's eyes and a large book underneath his arm. "Have you been in the library all this time?"

"Aye, Yir Grace," Orlynd said between heavy breaths.

Déor lowered his sword. "I'm relieved you are well. I take it you have been successful in identifying the creature that has been attacking us?"

"Aye, Yir Grace," Orlynd answered. "It is important Ah speak wi yis."

Déor nodded. "I am pleased. However, an audience shall have to wait until later. My castle is under attack, and I must help defend it. Please, leave the book here and accompany me. I must request the use of your wand skills once again."

As they passed the queen's chambers, the door opened and a very sleepy Anya stepped out. "What is going on, Déor? Why all the noise?"

Déor looked to his queen and said simply, "That is what I intend to find out."

CHAPTER SEVEN

COINNEACH CASTLE—
THE KINGDOM OF VANDOLAY
1248 CE

Exiting the castle onto the main courtyard, Déor and Orlynd were drawn up short. The scene before them was utter devastation. Remnants of wooden barrels burning could be seen in the distance. Several bodies lay about the grounds, the injured and the dead. They could also see the clothing of some of the bodies on fire. Whatever battle that had taken place had come to a termination.

"Notify the court physician. Those who are still alive will need to be relocated into our sanatorium in order to be properly treated."

"Aye, Yir Grace," Orlynd answered.

"Meet me in my private apartment later," Déor said, watching Orlynd nod his head before turning back toward the castle.

Next, the king came upon an injured guard. A fire lance lay beside him. He could see the guard's leg had been torn off at the knee and blood was quickly pooling beneath it.

Déor bent down to try to stop the bleeding.

"What happened here?" Déor asked.

"Our weapons," the guard gasped, "were useless against it."

"Against what? Explain!"

"There was…a monster!" The guard grimaced, breathing heavily. "I wielded my fire lance. I took aim at the creature and took my shot. I hit it. I know I did! I heard it scream. Next thing I knew the barrel, containing potassium nitrate, adjacent to the monster erupted, and it was bearing down upon us. It killed all the sentries nearby. My projectiles and the added flame did absolutely nothing!"

"And where is it now?"

"It flew off in the direction of Cara Forest."

Déor struggled to hide his frustration and instead decided to focus on the guard. "Please, tell me your name."

"Darius. Darius McKellen, sire," the guard said.

"You did well, Darius. Your bravery will not be forgotten."

"Thank you, sire," he said, his breathing becoming more uneven.

"Darius?" Déor said, noticing the guard taking a few last shuttering breaths.

"Sire," he whispered. "Forgive me." He then bent his head back and took his last breath.

"There is nothing to forgive. You have served me well," he answered, tears forming in his eyes.

MCKINNON ESTATE—
GLENDALOW
1248 CE

MIERTA, SITTING at a small writing desk in his father's bedroom, turned the page of a herbology book and read:

"Herbal Militaris—a multipurpose perennial that contains flower heads consisting of tiny, tightly packed floras found in shades of yellow, red, or pink."

He suddenly stopped and looked up from the book, distracted by what sounded like a piece of wood being hit against one of the trees near the front of the estate. After listening again for the sound, and hearing nothing, he went back to the book.

"This herb can be used to treat various illnesses and ailments such as digestion issues, lowering of fevers, nosebleeds, open-wound injuries, colds," he read out loud. He stopped again when he heard the noise. "Oh, for the love of peace!" He sighed and rubbed his temples in an attempt to soothe his ongoing headache. "I cannot possibly concentrate with these interruptions and find a proper remedy for the Shreya."

He stood from his chair and walked over to the window, placing his hands on the sill before he peered out, his brow furrowing.

"You fool," Mierta said, unable to believe the sight that had met his eyes. Lochlann was outside beating a tree with a wooden sword. And not simply any tree, either; it was the tree that Mierta and his father had planted as a memorial to his mother!

Quickly, Mierta ran down the hall to his bedroom and grabbed a wooden sword he used for practicing sword fighting before proceeding outside in an effort to stop Lochlann from doing any further damage.

"What are you doing?" Mierta yelled as he approached Lochlann, holding the wooden sword in his hand. "Why are you trying to destroy Mum's tree?"

"Sorry? What?" Lochlann stopped and looked back to assess the damage. There were marks throughout various branches of the tree. Shocked, he dropped his sword. "Sorry! I'm so sorry! I didn't...I mean, I didn't mean to. I was bored. I wasn't thinking."

"That's right. You're such a blubbering buffoon! You *never* think!" Mierta accused.

Lochlann's cheeks flushed and he began to stare down at the ground in shame.

Mierta raised his wooden sword. "Hit me."

"I'm sorry, what?" Lochlann said, looking up, confused.

"You heard me. Hit me! I dare say you've been wanting to ever since your Rite of Wands," Mierta said. "Go on, then. Do it."

As soon as Lochlann picked his wooden sword up from the ground, Mierta swung his first blow. "Come on, Mierta. Be fair," Lochlann said, blocking Mierta's sword.

"Fair? Are you implying that taking your frustration out on that tree is what's reasonable?" he said, swinging again at Lochlann, this time aiming for his head.

Again, Lochlann blocked. "No, but I know you'll simply wave your hand and cast a spell to make this tree come to life."

"Don't be ridiculous. I can't cast magic on any inanimate object. That would be cheating. Besides, I reckon what you really need is a worthier opponent capable of defending himself. Come on, you coward," Mierta said. "HIT ME!"

"Argh!" Lochlann cried as he charged forward, going for Mierta's elbow.

Mierta easily dodged Lochlann's manoeuvre.

"Not bad, little brother. I dare say you've picked up the skill of swordsmanship," Mierta said.

They squared up once more. This time Mierta advanced with a cry and thrust his sword at Lochlann's middle. Lochlann easily dodged Mierta's advance, twisted around, and thrust his sword behind him. The sword caught Mierta between the legs, causing Mierta to go down with agony.

"Don't you ever call me a coward!" Lochlann shouted at his older brother.

"*That* was most certainly unfair!" Mierta responded, gasping between painful breaths.

Lochlann looked down. He decided to give Mierta a final warning. He walked up to him and kicked him in the chest, knocking him onto his back. He pointed his sword down at Mierta's throat. "I dare say, big brother, you should leave the swordsmanship to me or..."

THE RITE OF ABNEGATION

"Or, what? Are you threatening me, Lochlann? Lochlann?" Mierta inquired as Lochlann turned his back and walked back toward the estate.

MCKINNON ESTATE— GLENDALOW 1248 CE

"LORD MCKINNON?" Armand called that evening from the parlour.

"I'm upstairs, Armand, in my father's bedroom," Mierta answered between flipping pages. He had managed to get through about half a book on herbology, having to occasionally transcribe a note or two for remembrance later.

After Armand walked in carrying a tray containing a bowl of stew and a cup of tea, he placed it on the desk beside the book Mierta was reading.

Mierta continued talking while keeping his eyes transfixed on the book. "You know, Armand, this book on herbology is brilliant. Absolutely brilliant! Have a case of the sniffles? There's an herb for that. Upset stomach? Leaves of the herbal militaris can be brewed into a tea. In pain? Use some of the bark of a willow tree." He closed the book. "Shame there isn't anything to mute a tongue."

"Monsieur?"

"You know precisely what I'm referring to," Mierta said with a sneer.

During his recent apprenticeship, Mierta learned through Master Ezekiel's daughter, Zorina, of a secret area, like a museum, in the kingdom of Aracelly that was designated for confiscated wands of witches and warlocks who had been forced to endure the Rite of Abnegation. It was strictly forbidden by Lord Kaeto for any witch or warlock to go there. Because Armand reported Mierta to Master Ezekiel after overhearing him discussing plans to investigate with Zorina's assistance, Mierta was unable to follow through.

When Master Ezekiel learned of Mierta's plans, he threatened to turn Mierta over to Lord Kaeto, who, Ezekiel was confident, would force the warlock to go through the Rite of Abnegation for his perceived wrongdoing. Even though that had occurred about ten years prior, Mierta had never forgiven Armand for his betrayal, therefore destroying any friendship he had with his father's servant. Armand was now his enemy, and Mierta was determined he would one day discover the consequences.

Mierta eyed the bowl suspiciously and briefly sniffed its contents. "What is in that anyway? It isn't poison, is it? I reckon it's some kind of stew."

"Oui. It is stew made from the meat of two squirrels," Armand said, ignoring Mierta's condescending tone.

"Squirrel stew?" Mierta said, impressed. "Blimey! I didn't know you knew how to clean squirrel."

"I don't. Lochlann assisted me in the kitchen."

"Ah." Mierta raised an eyebrow. "Did he now?" he muttered under his breath, still smarting from his loss to Lochlann. "At least he's good for something." He looked back at his herbology book, silently dismissing Armand.

Suddenly, there was a thud against the same window Mierta had been peering out of when he caught Lochlann beating his mother's tree. Looking up, he saw a smudge on the once clean window.

"What?" he muttered to himself, getting up to investigate and find what made the noise.

Mierta opened the window and looked out, seeing a courier pigeon laying on the grass. Its grey-and-white wings were still outstretched as if in flight. Its head was bent at an odd angle and its beak was bloody.

"Daft bird must have flown full force into the window!"

Further inspection revealed a note tied to its leg.

"Oh. Well, I suppose at least it didn't break the window."

COINNEACH CASTLE—
THE KINGDOM OF VANDOLAY
1248 CE

MY SON, *Mierta,*

I write to you in a time of peril. The kingdom is under attack. Not by any enemy yet known to us, but by a creature so foul, it can only be described as coming from the deepest depths of hell. Since our weapons have proven to be useless, all our efforts to be rid of it have thus failed. I have set a small apothecary within the castle with items I was able to gather from the marketplace. Despite this, I have been unable to keep up with the injured and dying. I beg of you; your assistance is required. The king is doing all he can to assist me, but he has no knowledge of healing, and I am limited in what I can teach him. Please! Make haste my son! Time is of the essence. May our dear Lord be with us all now!

In hope and desperation,
Your father

CHAPTER EIGHT

MCKINNON ESTATE—
GLENDALOW
1248 CE

Mierta made his way down the stairs, heading in the direction of the entryway before stopping directly in front of the oversized bogwood door with a cast-iron latch that led to the cellar. Reaching into his breeches pocket, he jingled the old-fashioned, rustic key with his hand for assurance before pulling it out and placing it into the keyhole, turning it anti-clockwise until he heard the bolt slide away.

"Yes!" he exclaimed, pleased he had managed to unlock it the first time around.

He pulled the door toward him as it opened with a loud creak. A familiar musty, mildewed aroma filled his nostrils, and an intense, cool draft emerged from below.

"Mmm. Home sweet home," he said with a grin.

Mierta put the key back in his pocket and grasped his wand.

"Scamos lias!" Mierta commanded as a dim turquoise, florescent light sparkled from the tip, revealing the cobblestone walls and stairs of the cellar.

"Right. There's no telling what kind of ailments or situations I may run into. Best to be prepared and gather as much as I can," he spoke to the air before stepping down on the first stair and closing the door behind him.

× ✕ ×

"MIERTA?" LOCHLANN called from the top of the cellar staircase. He could hear what sounded like someone rummaging around below. Then he heard a muffled bang.

"Ouch!" Mierta yelped, hitting his head on the cabinet while reaching for an empty flask. He dropped it carefully into his satchel. "Yes, I'm down here."

Mierta could hear Lochlann's footsteps echoing against the wall as he ventured down the stairs.

"Armand told me you were leaving," Lochlann said.

"Did he now?" Mierta asked, perplexed, his back facing his brother. Armand had supposedly left the room after handing Mierta the note from the ill-fated courier pigeon. "Why, yes. Father sent me a pigeon with an urgent message to come assist. There's some kind of trouble going on in the kingdom of Vandolay, and they're really struggling with the lot."

"Oh," Lochlann said.

Mierta turned to him and smiled. "Fancy coming along?"

"Me? Why? I don't know my way around there."

"Oh, I don't know," Mierta jested. "There's swords and sword fighting! Reckon a guard may be willing to provide you a lesson or two." He winked.

"Really? Why, that would be brilliant!" Lochlann said before his expression turned solemn.

"What? What is it? What's wrong?" Mierta asked, confused.

Lochlann nervously shifted his weight. He was uncertain whether he should ask his brother about the image he saw in his Rite of Wands, yet it was important to know.

"You've been to the kingdom of Vandolay with father before, correct?" Lochlann asked.

"Yes. Found it very boring, except for when I accidentally bumped into the queen, but that's another story. Why? You don't fancy to come?" Mierta said, noticing Lochlann's hesitation.

Lochlann was transported back to his Rite of Wands ceremony. He found himself inside a circular room. The walls were made of chiselled stone. There were two small windows near the ceiling that let in the cool, salty sea air. Heavy brocade cloth was hanging loose at the sides, gently swaying in the breeze. Between these windows was a shelf with various items that Lochlann barely noticed. The floor was bare wood planks that had been polished over time by many boot falls. The only other escape out of the room was through a door that was attached to a staircase, which led to the ground level.

"Seawater," Lochlann abruptly muttered, returning to the present. "Is the kingdom of Vandolay located near the sea?"

"What?" Mierta asked, confused. "Oh, no, no. Coinneach Castle is closest to Cara Forest. It's a forest with lots and lots of red leaves and wildlife. Why? Were you hoping to slay a fish with a sword?" Mierta laughed at the thought.

"No, but…"

"If you'd rather stay here with Armand, that's all right. Simply thought I'd offer."

"I'll come with you!" Lochlann announced.

Mierta smiled, pleased. "Splendid. Go quickly and pack your belongings."

COINNEACH CASTLE—
THE KINGDOM OF VANDOLAY
1248 CE

THAT EVENING, Déor stared out the window in the direction of the castle's gardens and fields, lost in his own thoughts of despair. His thoughts were interrupted when he heard several loud knocks at the door of his private apartment.

He sighed, turning his gaze toward the door. "Yes?"

Thomas's armour clanked against the wooden floor as he opened the door.

"Your Grace," Thomas said, bowing. "The warlock—"

"Thank you, Thomas," Déor said, interrupting his guard as he continued to stare out the window. "Please, send Orlynd in and close the door behind you."

"Aye, Your Grace," Thomas said, standing aside to allow Orlynd to enter the king's private apartment.

Orlynd lowered his gaze toward the ground, bowed and positioned his hands inside his brown robe as he entered the king's chambers.

The thick, richly decorated rug stretching from wall-to-wall muffled his footsteps as he entered. The appearance inside the private apartment hadn't changed much since Déor had been crowned king.

Heavy royal red drapes hung from the top of the two floor-to-ceiling windows, which had been pulled back. Several windows hung open to allow a slight breeze to cool the room. The sparse furnishings included two writing desks and chairs made of a dark walnut wood. There was also a quartet of floor-to-ceiling shelves, filled with books, on either side of a doorway at the far end of the room. Orlynd took notice of a table that had previously held wooden soldiers and ships set strategically for battle. They had been replaced by a chess set, with all the white pieces scattered amongst the board like fallen soldiers. King Déor stood with his back to the room, looking out the window.

"At the end of February," Déor began sullenly, "this field will be filled with beautiful purple-and-white crocuses as far as the eye can see. I pray we shall survive long enough to see them bloom again."

"Yis shall," Orlynd answered confidently.

"Not if I don't find a way to defeat the enemy first. Tell me, what have you discovered about it?"

Orlynd recalled the large illustration of the creature from the encyclopaedia. "It is called the Sulchyaes."

"Sulchyaes," Déor repeated. "Why have I never heard of this creature before?"

"It's a devilish creature, believed tae huv been conjured by druids."

"Are you saying this creature was created by magic?" Déor said, shocked and angered.

"Aye," Orlynd answered. "Dark magic, Ah reckon. It has the head ay a Krampus, a body ay a lion, claws ay an eagle, wings ay a black bird, n the tail ay a snake."

"If what you say is true, then why doesn't the kingdom of Aracelly come to our aid, specifically your leader?"

"Lord Kaeto dinnae like tae interfere. But Ah can assure yis, it will nae go unnoticed. If he has nae been informed he soon will be."

"Is there no way to defeat it?"

"Nae by weapons made by men. It would be best tae be rid ay it wi dark magic."

"And this is something you cannot do?"

"Nay, Yir Grace."

Déor raised his hand in the air and clenched it. He lowered it slowly and sat in a chair near the chess set, taking a moment to gather his thoughts. "I feel like I'm losing control of my own kingdom and I am unable to protect it. How many survived the latest attack?"

"None, Yir Grace," Orlynd replied sadly. "The court physician has done whit he can, but it is impossible wi the ongoing attacks."

"That I am aware," the king answered, short-tempered, cutting Orlynd off. "Then, I fear there is only one thing left to do." Déor stood up from his chair and began to walk toward the doorway of his private apartment.

"Where r yis going?" Orlynd asked.

"To seek out my queen," Déor answered, stopping once he reached the door. He turned his head. "I shall go visit her in her chambers and express my love for her. Our kingdom is in peril and it is important to demonstrate to the subjects the crown is strong and shall survive. There has been increased uncertainty of this amongst my people because Anya has not been able to produce a child. Even if I shall perish, I can only pray that God may allow my lineage to be capable of continuing by blessing our union with a son. Therefore, she must be protected. I have decided to make arrangements for Anya to visit my hand, her father in Glendalow. She shall remain there until it is confirmed this creature has been defeated."

× ✕ ×

MY DEAREST *father,*

I am pleased to send you this message ahead of my arrival. I shall be bringing with me some additional healing herbs and potions from the cellar that may come of use. I am certain they cannot be found in the king's stores nor the marketplace.

Lochlann shall also be accompanying me. I believe he will benefit from experiencing everyday life in the kingdom of men and find the sword skills of the king's soldiers fascinating.

Please send my apologies to the king. The pigeon he sent had an unfortunate accident and is dead. I suppose Armand will find some use for its carcass.

Your most obedient son,
Mierta

CHAPTER NINE

COINNEACH CASTLE—
THE KINGDOM OF VANDOLAY
1248 CE

One week later, Mierta opened his eyes, finding himself in the upstairs bedroom of the small apothecary his father had been given by the king. It had been a long, tiring week of helping his father take care of the injured because of the continuing attacks from the Sulchyaes. He sat up, noticing Lochlann's empty bed.

I wonder where he's wandered off to. Perhaps he's with Father in the sanatorium.

Mierta raised stiffly off the rough straw mattress. He stretched his tired muscles, retrieved his satchel from the floor, and headed down the warped wooden staircase. Entering the small room, he glanced around it in disgust.

Nothing like home at all. Would have thought better from a castle!

The room was somewhat square shaped with a window on two sides and a door on another. The wall opposite the door held shelves filled with books and vials containing remedies of various sorts. There was a cookstove in one corner that was still warm, from breakfast Mierta supposed. In the centre of the room stood a rough wooden table and chairs. Mierta's eyes brightened a bit. A woven basket full of fruit sat on the table. He grabbed a big apple and took a bite.

"This will do for me, for now. Right. Back to work!" he said to himself as he headed out of the apothecary toward the direction of the sanitorium located inside the castle.

As he opened the door to the sanitorium and entered, he watched the utter chaos that met his eyes. Last night's attack had taken its toll. People were running here and there around the sparsely furnished room, helping where they could, changing blood-soaked bandages, offering drinks of water or retrieving blankets as needed. There were cots and mattresses arranged along the walls, each holding an injured soldier. Simple small tables were clustered in the centre of room to keep bowls of water and remedies close at hand. At the far end of the room stood a large wardrobe that contained clean linens, bandages, and simple potions for the more common ailments. Its doors hung open and bandages hung haphazardly off the shelves.

Mierta caught a glimpse of his father in the middle of the melee and had begun to make his way toward him, gingerly stepping over piles of soiled bandages and weaving around people, when he heard one of the soldiers on a nearby cot moaning a request for water. Turning, Mierta noticed a pitcher of water near the bed. He immediately walked over, dipped a large ladle into the water, grasped the bottom, and gently placed it to the soldier's mouth so he could drink. After the man was finished, he placed the ladle back on the small table next to the pitcher.

"Mierta, my dear boy," Mortain said, startling his son. "I was getting worried. You do not normally appear this late."

"Father," Mierta said. He took the opportunity to gaze around the room for any signs of Lochlann before responding. "I'm sorry. I must have overslept. Have you seen Lochlann?"

"No," Mortain answered. "I reckoned he was with you."

"Oh, I do hope he didn't go get himself lost. It took me two days to navigate this place. Perhaps then it would be best to have a look for him."

"I'm sure Lochlann can take care of himself," Mortain said. "I reckon you don't need me to tell you how badly you are needed here."

"Yes, Father," Mierta said, crinkling his brow.

COINNEACH CASTLE—
THE KINGDOM OF VANDOLAY
1248 CE

"RIGHT, YOU miserable lot," Aindrias said, addressing the three nervous sentries standing on the side of the training yard, dressed and ready for battle. "Here's your chance to show you've got what it takes to survive an attack by the Sulchyaes. His Majesty has permitted me to put you all through a test of endurance involving sword fighting to prove your worthiness."

Aindrias, the king's guard, watched as the sentries took up positions around him. He turned in a circle, looking at each one, waiting for one to advance in attack. He didn't have to wait long. One of the sentries behind his back raised his practice sword high above his head and advanced with a cry. Aindrias whirled around, raised his shield and deflected the attack, causing the man to stumble past him. He then brought his own sword around and hit the attacker square between the shoulder blades, knocking the air out of his lungs and felling him to the ground.

The second sentry advanced at Aindrias and was summarily dealt with. The last one standing took a different approach. Having seen his fellows dealt with so quickly he weighed his options and decided on a frontal approach. He advanced on Aindrias slowly with his shield and sword at the ready. They stared at each other while slowly circling. The sentry thrust his sword forward and it was quickly deflected off Aindrias's shield. The sentry went for a low attack at Aindrias's legs. Aindrias sidestepped the sword, swung around and quickly brought his own sword soundly down on the sentry's head, knocking him out.

"Fat lot of use you three were. Guess what? If this had been a real attack, you'd all be dead!" Aindrias said over the painful moans from those still on the ground. "Now, get your lazy butts off the ground, and let's do this again. On your feet!"

As the sentries proceeded to stand up, Aindrias noticed out of the corner of his eye what appeared to be a young warlock standing near one of the wooden fences, watching them. He smirked. "Oh, look, lads. I reckon we have got ourselves an admirer," Aindrias said, walking over to him.

"I don't suppose you're planning on interfering with our engagement and embarrassing me in front of the sentries, warlock?"

"What?" Lochlann asked, confused, before realising what Aindrias was implying. "No, I don't use magic."

Aindrias laughed. "What kind of rubbish is that? I've never heard of a warlock not capable of practicing magic."

"It's true. I don't!" Lochlann said.

"Really? Then, may I inquire what you're really doing here, then? I cannot imagine you possibly have any interest in what those jumped-up dung beetles are doing," Aindrias said with a smile, turning to the sentries standing around waiting for another opportunity to engage with him.

"I know how to fight," Lochlann said, raising a sword containing a three-foot wooden blade toward Aindrias.

Aindrias turned and observed the sword's blade, handle, guard, and wheel pommel. "You can't be serious?" He laughed.

"My brother said you may permit me to join," Lochlann said.

"Join?" He turned toward the sentries with disbelief. "This warlock has decided to insult us by making a mockery with this feeble wooden sword of his."

"No, no, that's not true. I only wish to be permitted to spar and perfect my skill," Lochlann said, pleading.

Aindrias gave a cruel, little laugh that was echoed by the sentries. "Get off with you now! This is the serious business of men, not the mere games of boys! Go back to the kingdom of Aracelly and play with your wand. Our kingdom is in need of protecting, and I refuse to allow your distractions to delay us any further."

Lochlann started to protest, but Aindrias simply kicked dust and gravel at him and turned his back. Lochlann was met with even more laughs from the others around. Embarrassed at having been made fun of, he turned in the opposite direction and started running. He didn't know where he was going nor did he care; he had to get away from there.

CARA FOREST—
THE KINGDOM OF VANDOLAY
1248 CE

LOCHLANN WANDERED around for some time before arriving at the conclusion he was lost. Turning down another path, he came upon an area that he had never seen before. A grass-covered path stretched out before him. The forest trees had formed a seemingly never-ending tunnel with their branches, and the leaves and moss gave off a green hue, lending an eerie atmosphere to it. Uncertain if he should continue onward, he took in a deep breath, letting it out before pressing on.

The trees seemed to close around him as he walked into the tunnel they formed. It was comforting and disconcerting at the same time. Something about this place called to him, though he couldn't understand exactly why.

As he continued forward, he spotted a man a short distance up the path. The man was fair skinned with shoulder-length, wavy red hair. He stood half a head taller than Lochlann and wore leggings of a dark material, which Lochlann was unfamiliar with, along with a brown-coloured shirt. Over his shoulder was a large bag.

Curious. I wonder what he's doing alone all the way out here? Maybe he would know the way back to the castle? I shall approach him and find out.

However, before he could get close to the man, he abruptly stopped in his tracks. The man was not alone.

Standing exactly off the path was a large, terrifying creature! It appeared to be at least twice the height of the man. As Lochlann swallowed hard, he observed the creature had the head of a Krampus, a body of a lion, claws of an eagle, wings of a black bird, and the tail of a snake.

Then, the man caught a glimpse of Lochlann out of the corner of his eye. He smiled smugly and proceeded to reach into the bag hanging on his shoulder, revealing a rather large fish. The creature let out an ear-piercing cry that sounded like an adult eagle's call. The man tossed the fish into the air, and the creature jumped up and caught it firmly in its jaws before proceeding to tear into its flesh for a snack.

"Fascinating creature, don't you reckon?" the man said as he turned toward Lochlann.

Lochlann swallowed hard and nodded, watching the man approach.

"My name is Tarik. Tarik Fuller. And, you are?"

"Lochlann. Lochlann McKinnon," he said, his voice breaking.

"McKinnon?" Tarik said with surprise, recognising the surname. "Wouldn't have expected the son of the court physician to be permitted to wander off on his own in these woods."

"I'm not," Lochlann corrected. "I got lost."

He didn't wish to go into how he had gotten bored watching his brother and father treat injured and dying people, and in the process of walking the castle's grounds, he came across a couple of the king's guards engaged in a duel. He remembered Mierta's proposal of a guard possibly allowing him to sword fight, but when he inquired, he was laughed at and bullied by Aindrias and other guards. Heart-broken, he ran aimlessly into Cara Forest, only to realise he couldn't find his way out.

"Hmm. Is that so?" Tarik laughed. "That's not really a surprise. This forest can be tricky to manoeuvre if you don't know your way around."

"Is that...that...thing," Lochlann stuttered, "what's been attacking the guards in the kingdom of Vandolay?"

"Thing? This is no thing; its name is the Sulchyaes. There's no need to be afraid of it. He won't hurt you unless I tell him to. And I reckon you wouldn't want me to set him upon you, am I correct?"

"Yes, but why?" Lochlann asked, growing uneasy. "Why are you allowing it to hurt all of those people?"

"You would too if the king sent your father to Tarloch to be tortured to death."

"I don't understand," Lochlann said.

"Of course, you wouldn't. You probably weren't even born when the king's father died," Tarik said. "One of my father's servants was accused of treason. And when he was arrested, the crown came for my dad. Neither of them were ever heard in court. Instead, they were both sent to Castle Tarloch."

"And they didn't come out?" Lochlann said, growing more uneasy.

"Fool! Don't you know that no one who is imprisoned in Castle Tarloch ever comes out alive?"

"I'm sorry, I didn't," Lochlann said, watching as Tarik proceeded to reach into the bag hanging on his shoulder, revealing another rather large fish. "Hang on," Lochlann stopped suddenly, suspicion creeping into his mind, "how are you able to command it? It's a wild creature."

The Sulchyaes again let out an ear-piercing cry before Tarik tossed the fish into the air. "Blimey, how else do you reckon I can?" Tarik said, not expecting an answer as the Sulchyaes jumped up and caught it firmly in its jaws. "I conjured it using black magic. The kingdom has all kinds of books about black magic in their restriction section that they don't want warlocks knowing about."

Lochlann's face went white. "You're a warlock?"

Tarik laughed. "You really are an idiot. Do I honestly look like a simple man to you? Pathetic." He reached into his bag and pulled out a Gabon ebony wand with an elegant tulip-shape design at the handle and a moldavite crystal connected at the shaft.

Lochlann froze. The wand reminded him of his brother's.

"Ah. Familiar with my wand's abilities I see," Tarik acknowledged.

"My brother's wand is crafted of the same material as yours."

"Is that so? Shame he's not with you. I would have liked to have faced an opponent with similar qualities. Do be sure to tell him if you should be lucky and actually survive."

"What do you mean?" Lochlann asked, taking a step backwards.

Tarik laughed. "Well, it has been a lovely chat, but I'm afraid this is where things end. I can't have you go back to the king and blubber all about me now, can I?"

"I won't tell anyone. I promise. You can trust me. It'll be our secret."

"Hmm. I appreciate your word, but I can't risk you slipping. However, what I can assure you of is that my beast will make your death swift, exactly like the others."

"What? No, please! I don't want to die; if a fight with my brother is what you want, then it'll happen. Give me the chance to…"

"Sulchyaes, attack!" Tarik shouted, pointing his arm out toward Lochlann.

Lochlann grasped his wand, pulled it out of his robe, and pointed it toward the Sulchyaes, desperately searching his memory for any spell to save himself. He could feel his heart throbbing in his chest as he found himself looking up into the face of the terrifying creature. It growled as it advanced; then, with a mighty flap of its wings, it extended its talons and attacked.

The last thing he remembered before losing consciousness was hearing the sound of his own screaming, along with the feeling of unbearable pain as his body was ripped into by the creature.

CHAPTER TEN

COINNEACH CASTLE—
THE KINGDOM OF VANDOLAY
1248 CE

Mortain entered the throne room and made his way to Déor before bowing. Torches burned silently between the large pillars that lined the great hall. Ornate tapestries hung from the tops of the pillars like silent sentries. On the walls behind the pillars were floor-to-ceiling stained glass windows that were darkened now that it was night. A large, open fire pit, in the very centre of the hall, was filled with burning wood, heating the room. He took note of Déor sitting on the throne with an empty chair next to him. The king looked rather displeased.

"Court physician, it is my belief you have a good reason for requesting an audience at this late hour?" Déor sneered.

"Yes, Your Grace," Mortain said. "My son has gone missing."

"Your son?" Déor asked, confused. He looked momentarily at Mierta, who was standing beside his father, before turning back to his court physician. "I do not follow. Explain."

"My younger brother, Lochlann, is missing," Mierta chimed in. "He hasn't been seen by me or my father since early this morning. It is not like him to go wandering off on his own. He's only twelve! I fear he may be in grave danger."

"I see," Déor said.

"I request, if I may, a guard or two to help look for my son. Mierta and I have been unable to take ourselves away from those sick and injured," Mortain said.

Déor gave a short mirthless laugh. "Are you suggesting I freely offer my guards up to the Sulchyaes? As you are aware, our numbers are dangerously depleted. I cannot spare even one and take the chance he may be killed."

"But Your Majesty," Mortain cried, his heart sinking, "I beg of you! My son is defenceless."

"It is to my understanding he is a warlock, is he not? He should be capable of handling danger, shouldn't he?"

"My father speaks the truth!" Mierta interjected. "While my brother may be a warlock, he refuses to wield his wand. He has no interest in casting magic."

"Regardless, I still cannot grant your request without leaving my kingdom defenceless; however, I will have my servants inquire if anyone has come across a young warlock of his description. I'm sure you understand the position I am in?"

"Yes, Your Grace. Thank you," Mortain said.

"Yes, well, if there's nothing further, I bid you both a good night. I shall pray for your son's well-being."

Mortain and Mierta bowed to the king as he left the room. Then they returned to the sanitorium to continue looking after the injured soldiers.

COINNEACH CASTLE—
THE KINGDOM OF VANDOLAY
1248 CE

"YOUR GRACE," Aindrias said, bowing before the king the following morning. Sunlight shone brightly in the throne room through a large, round window above the entrance. The sunspot it left on the floor matched its intricate design.

"Thank you, Aindrias, for coming. A recent urgent matter has come to my attention, which requires your assistance."

"Yes, Your Grace?" Aindrias said, a bit confused.

Déor stood from his throne and slowly walked down to his guard. "The son of my court physician has gone missing. My servants' inquiries indicate you know of his whereabouts."

Aindrias swallowed hard, feeling the king's eyes on him.

"Eh, not exactly, Your Grace," Aindrias answered nervously.

Déor gave his guard a stern look. "Explain."

Aindrias looked at the wall beyond Déor, unable to meet his king's eyes. "I was training the sentries in the practice yard. I had only finished sparring when I noticed the young warlock standing near the fence. The buffoon thought he would be able to join us. Claimed he wouldn't even use magic." Aindrias paused, looking to Déor for understanding of how absurd this was.

Déor simply raised his eyebrows and encouraged Aindrias to continue.

Aindrias cleared his throat. "Um…well…I may have discouraged the warlock a bit too harshly. I told him to get lost. Last I saw of him, he was running off toward the forest. I didn't take notice of him again for the remainder of the time I was with the sentries."

"The forest," Déor said, pacing behind his guard. "Cara Forest. The precise location where the Sulchyaes had been seen flying toward the previous night?"

"Aye, Your Grace," Aindrias said more nervously.

Déor, who had now moved in front of his guard, raised his hand before clenching it in a fist. "You lubber wort! For your punishment you shall spend the rest of the day and night in the stocks."

"But, sire!" Aindrias protested.

"And, I suggest you pray to whatever God you pray to he comes back alive. Otherwise, I'll have no choice but to liberate your head from your shoulders with my own sword. How can I expect my court physician to give his undivided attention to our injured when he must worry about his son?"

"Guards!" Déor shouted as Thomas approached through the doors, two other guards accompanying him.

Déor pointed to the two guards with Thomas. "Take Aindrias to the stocks. No matter how much he begs, do not free him until the morrow."

"Yes, Your Grace," the guards said as they restrained Aindrias before dragging him away. Aindrias opened his mouth to protest then silently closed it, knowing anything more would simply anger the king further.

"Thomas, see to it that Mierta and Orlynd are summoned for an audience immediately. It's going to be a long day," Déor said before retaking a seat on his throne.

COINNEACH CASTLE—
THE KINGDOM OF VANDOLAY
1248 CE

ORLYND HAD only finished consuming a small breakfast when he heard an abrupt, loud knock at the door.

Ah wonder who that wid be. Ah dinnae recall inviting anybody, Orlynd thought before putting on a dressing gown and opening the door.

On the other side was a young man barely in his teens. He had a brown cap on over his shaved head. He was wearing a short-sleeved, light blue, woollen tunic over a dark blue long-sleeved shirt. His breeches were beige in colour with dark blue socks that stretched up to his thighs, and his shoes were made of a simple leather footwear, most often seen in court rather than out on the streets. A leather satchel hung at his side.

"A letter from His Majesty the king. He seeks an audience with you at once," the royal messenger said, handing the letter over to Orlynd.

"Ah thank yis," Orlynd said before closing the door. Quickly reading over the letter, he realised he was expected in the king's throne room within a few minutes!

Blimey! How am Ah supposed tae explain ma delay tae the king?

After quickly dressing, Orlynd raced out the door and started to make his way through town in the direction of the castle grounds. He passed by several carts and booths that were being restocked for the day's market. As he continued to make his way, his mind became preoccupied with the reasons the king might have called this audience. When he heard a shout coming from above, he looked up to see what looked like the bottom of a chamber pot. Realising what was about to occur, he jumped out of the way as the path he had been walking on was showered with refuse from a latrine.

Thit was close, Orlynd thought.

He coughed, swinging his hand back and forth, trying to rid the area of the foul air that had suddenly intruded.

"Get out of the road!" a young man abruptly warned from his carriage, forcing Orlynd to jump back onto the path, barely escaping being run down.

"Blimey!"

It was then that his luck ran out. Before Orlynd knew what was happening, he found himself doused with a mixture of solid and liquid waste.

"Oh, gen up!" he called out, shaking his fist at the person who was now looking out the window and laughing at his expense. "The king will appreciate this!"

Not having time to return to the cottage and change his attire, Orlynd rubbed as much of the mess off his robe as he could before heading on to his audience. Before entering the throne room, he stopped, identifying the voice of the king discussing Cara Forest. Realising there was no way to prevent commotion from his entrance, he sighed and folded his robes over his shoulders to hide as much of the mess as he could. If anything, it would keep the stench down, he hoped. He quickly joined Mierta's side.

"Orlynd," Déor addressed, noticing his soothsayer had entered the room. "Nice of you to finally decide to join us."

"A thousand pardons, Yir Grace," Orlynd said as Mierta eyed him. "Ah'm afraid the messenger yis sent me arrived late."

"I see. Now, where were we?" Déor asked, regathering his thoughts.

"Your Grace," Mierta said. "I can't explain what in blazes made my brother think it was a good idea to wander off in there. Nonetheless, I offer my services to go to Cara Forest and have a proper look myself."

"Ah'll accompany yis," Orlynd said quickly. "Ah shall offer yis ma wand as protection."

Mierta shook his head. "I thank you for your offer, but I don't need protecting," Mierta answered. "I'm capable of handling things myself."

"I disagree," King Déor affirmed. "Whether you are capable of protecting yourself is not the point. I am obligated to provide you aid. Being the son of my kingdom's court physician, your life is extremely valuable. To all of us. Therefore, I have decided my soothsayer, Orlynd, shall accompany you."

"Aye, Yir Grace," Orlynd said.

The king continued. "Orlynd is both skilled in magic and familiar with the surroundings of Cara Forest." He turned his attention to his soothsayer. "Orlynd, will you swear to protect Mierta, and if it would come necessary, lay your life down for him as you would for me?"

Mierta turned and eyed Orlynd.

"Aye, Yir Grace."

"Then, it is settled—" The king stopped in mid-sentence after catching wind of the most offensive stench. He sniffed loudly. "What in God's good graces is that awful smell?"

Orlynd's cheeks flushed. He cleared his throat and stared at the floor. "Eh. Ah'm sorry, Yir Grace."

The king blinked in disbelief. "Orlynd. When I said to have a look at the stalls, I didn't mean to literally sleep in them!"

"Ah dinnae, Yir Grace. A commoner dumped a latrine pot oan me!" Orlynd answered. When he noticed the shock displayed on Déor's face, he turned to stare back down at the ground. "S-sorry, Yir Grace."

Mierta turned to Orlynd, finding it difficult to keep a straight face.

"Do check with my servants and find yourself a change of attire before you make your leave."

Orlynd answered sheepishly, "Aye, Yir Grace."

"Right, now that that fiasco is over, I shall resign to my private apartment for the remainder of the morning as I strategize the best option to rid this land of that evil creature. You may all leave me now and return to your business."

CHAPTER ELEVEN

CARA FOREST—
THE KINGDOM OF VANDOLAY
1248 CE

"L ochlann!" Mierta called into the forest, noticing the sun was starting to set between the trees. It was sundown and soon darkness would be their companion, making their search for Lochlann ever the more difficult. They had previously dismounted their horses and left them tied to a nearby tree, for the forest was getting too thick for them to continue.

Mierta pulled out his wand and continued forward, slowly, listening for any sound other than the crunching of leaves beneath his own feet before concluding the area was clear of imminent danger. They had been searching for him for what seemed like hours but had not come across any clues of where he may have wandered off to. Mierta was starting to feel doubt in his heart that they would be able to find him on what was left of the day, the second day he was missing.

"This ain," Orlynd suggested. "Thir's another area ay the forest, which leads toward the northern sections ay Iverna. Ah reckon Lochlann may huv tried this ain tae git tae Glendalow."

Mierta nodded and followed.

Shortly, the warlocks found themselves looking down a grass-covered path that stretched out before them. As Orlynd stared toward the forest trees making a seemingly never-ending tunnel with their branches, he grew ever more uneasy. Something didn't feel right.

Suddenly, he heard a weeping voice coming from an area in the trees plead, "Help me."

Orlynd's blood ran cold.

Slowly, he looked up and saw a white image of whom he assumed was Lochlann, free floating in the air. His arms were stretched outwards. There were large gashes through the material of his tunic and shirt, and blood had already begun seeping quickly through them, causing drops of blood to trickle onto the ground beneath them.

"Oh, ma dear Lord, Lochlann," Orlynd whispered.

"Lochlann? I'm sorry, what?" Mierta said, thinking he had heard Orlynd say his brother's name.

Abruptly the image of Lochlann screamed at them as Mierta passed underneath.

Startled, Orlynd realised he was really seeing the banshee using Lochlann's form, which meant that Lochlann's life was in great peril.

"Stop!" Orlynd shouted, reaching his arm out toward Mierta. The piercing cry from the banshee was tormenting. "Dinnae move any farther! We r nae alone."

Seeing the pained expression on Orlynd's face, Mierta crinkled his brow. "Why? What's wrong?"

Orlynd motioned with his hand as if to indicate to Mierta he should retract his steps.

Mierta obeyed and stood next to Orlynd. After watching Orlynd lower his arm, reach into his robe for his wand and lift it, Mierta did the same with his wand. Next, he followed Orlynd's glance, confused at what he was looking at, seeing nothing but trees and their branches.

"Sorry, but what are we supposed to be looking at?"

"The banshee," Orlynd answered.

"Pardon?" Mierta asked. "That's a story."

"Nay. Believe me, it's nae a story," Orlynd said. "The banshee is an omen, a devilish creature, appearing only tae those families who r cursed."

"Cursed?!"

"Aye," Orlynd said. "It is believed thir r five cursed families in Iverna—the O'Brien's, the O'Neill's, the O'Grady's, the O'Connor's, and the Kavanagh's."

"Master Ezekiel is of the Kavanagh family," Mierta uttered, wondering why the apothecarist never mentioned anything about the banshee.

"Aye," Orlynd confirmed. "The banshee appears tae us in times ay peril, tae deliver a warning."

"Warning?" Mierta said. "A warning about what?"

"Thit death is near fir someone ay great importance. The banshee can appear in any form but especially enjoys taunting, appearing as someone yis care about! Trust me, if yis could see whit Ah can right now, yis wid be reacting, tae."

He stepped forward exactly when Mierta's face displayed shock.

"Lochlann," Mierta uttered, tears filling his eyes. "Are you saying…that creature…has taken the form of my brother? She's come to warn you that he's dead?"

"Begone, yis foul creature!" Orlynd commanded, raising his wand. "Release him, n bother us nae more! Yis r nae permitted tae use his image!"

"Lochlann's dead? No. That can't be," Mierta whispered, feeling faint.

The banshee let out a shrieking cry as Orlynd cast, "*Klaocala!*"

The banshee transformed, disintegrating into a thick, white glue-like substance before exploding in the air, covering Orlynd's new robe with its substance. "Oh, gen up! Ah pray this be the last thing that happens tae me today. Though Ah suppose it is a good thing nobody else can see this. Goat tae git myself cleaned up before returning tae the castle, nonetheless."

"Lochlann!" Mierta cried, interrupting Orlynd's thoughts as he suddenly caught what looked like his brother lying unconscious, sprawled out on his back in the grass a bit farther up the path. He took off at a run and rushed over to his brother's side.

"Mierta! Come back!"

Mierta abruptly stopped once he had reached his brother's unconscious body. He could see Lochlann's right hand barely grasping his wand, limp at his side.

"Lochlann!" he whispered between breaths, recognising his brother's injuries were similar to the men's back at Coinneach Castle. "No! You encountered the Sulchyaes."

Crinkling his brow, he quickly put his wand away. There were large gashes through the material of his tunic from what looked like oversized talons.

"Lochlann," Mierta said desperately, kneeling down in the grass, cradling his brother's face in his hands. "Oh, please don't be dead. Wake up. Wake up, please."

With a trembling hand, he reached a finger up toward the side of Lochlann's neck, feeling for a pulse, fearing the worst.

"He's alive!" He breathed a sigh of relief before the difference in body temperature was comprehended. Mierta's eyes rapidly moved back and forth with concern as his mind raced. Hastily, he placed his hand over his brother's forehead to confirm. "Blimey! He's burning up. Wound fever. The symptoms can surface as quick as one day after sustaining injury. I need to lower his temperature."

Mierta could feel his own heart increase in pace as he searched his bag for a cloth. He then pulled the flask from around his shoulder, opened the cap and poured water onto the rag until it was full of moisture. He placed it over Lochlann's forehead.

"There, that should do for now. Right. Now onto his injuries."

Orlynd approached from the path and looked over at Lochlann, but Mierta ignored him. Taking in a deep breath, Mierta was careful not to grimace as he carefully separated his brother's blood-soaked clothing in order to determine how bad the injuries were. He gasped, noticing that under the gashes in Lochlann's tunic were deep bleeding wounds that needed to be sutured. Mierta watched as each quick breath Lochlann took only seemed to make more blood appear.

"I...I've got to do something. He'll die if...okay, Mierta, don't panic. Think!" His words were cut short when he was certain he could see something white shining through some of the wounds.

Blimey! Is that bone? No, no, it can't be! he thought to himself, his eyes filling with worry. *Oh, Lochlann. I'm so sorry! I should have never suggested you come here. This is all my fault.*

Looking down, Mierta's eyes went wide after noticing a significant amount of additional blood had already pooled at his brother's sides.

"Hang on, Lochlann," Mierta said with determination in his eyes. "Your big brother is here. I'm going to save you. Stay with me!"

"Whit r yis doing?" Orlynd asked, hovering to see if he could be of assistance.

"Lochlann's life is in peril. I need...I need," Mierta said, stopping. He brushed his hands through his hair as his mind raced. "A poultice. I need a paste! Something to slow down the bleeding. Argh!" He continued to search through his satchel. "I'm so incredibly stupid. If only I had studied healing magic in Poveglia like my grandad. I would have been able to help him right now with a restoration spell!"

"Mierta..." Orlynd said, trying to comfort.

"Aha!" Mierta exclaimed, abruptly pulling out a bottle of wine from his bag. "I wondered where this thing had gone off to. Shame no one is going to be able to drink it, but it will do." He grabbed the cork with his teeth and popped it off. Then, he stood over his brother and poured the liquid over Lochlann's chest.

Hearing Lochlann moan from the pain, Mierta crinkled his brow.

"I'm so sorry, Lochlann. I'm so terribly sorry. I know it hurts," he said, continuing to pour the liquid until the bottle was empty.

He was thankful when his brother appeared to fall unconscious.

Mierta looked up and turned to Orlynd. "Do you know of the location of any willow trees in this forest?"

"A willow tree?"

"Yes. I can use its bark to relieve my brother's pain. Also, we need more water to reduce his fever."

"Mierta," Orlynd said. "Git a hold ay yirself! Lochlann must be moved tae safety immediately n git him back tae the castle before the Sulchyaes returns."

It was exactly the call to action that Mierta needed. Orlynd was right; he couldn't heal his brother there, and they could all be in danger if the Sulchyaes returned.

There was a look of hate in Mierta's eyes when he looked back at the soothsayer. "I dare the Sulchyaes to return and face me," he said, lifting Lochlann into his arms and heading toward where they had left the horses. "And when it does, trust me. I will destroy it."

CHAPTER TWELVE

COINNEACH CASTLE—
THE KINGDOM OF VANDOLAY
1248 CE

"Make way! Make way!" Orlynd shouted as he and Mierta rushed up the stairs with Lochlann and down the hall toward the sanitorium—Mierta staring straight ahead as he cradled his brother in his arms.

Through all the chaos, the activity inside the castle seemed to momentarily cease as the sound of the commotion and people running in the hallway became louder through the sanitorium's door entrance.

Orlynd thrust his wand toward the door.

"*Obrate combriando!*" Orlynd cast, abruptly causing the door to slam open. He gestured for Mierta to step inside.

As Mierta entered the sanitorium, he frantically looked around the room. All of the cots were already occupied by other sick and injured soldiers, and his father was nowhere to be seen.

"You there," Mierta said, addressing a nurse who was finishing up changing the dressing of a wound. "Where's my father, the court physician? My brother is injured and needs immediate attention."

The nurse stood up from her chair, turned to Mierta and gasped, comprehending the grave situation.

"Oh, my good gracious!" She looked around the room, noticing a table filled with bandages, bowls of water and several bottles with various remedies in them. "Bring him over here," she advised.

He waited for the table to be cleaned before he laid an unconscious Lochlann down on it.

"My apologies. I'm afraid all the cots are full. The court physician went to deliver His Majesty a remedy for his insomnia. He's been complaining he hasn't been sleeping well since the creature started attacking. I expect he should return soon."

Orlynd leaned in to Mierta. "Ah'll go tae the king's private apartment, inform the king n find yir father. Yis concentrate oan taking care ay yir brother."

"Thank you." Mierta nodded, crinkling his brow. He turned to the nurse. "We found him in Cara Forest. He'd been attacked by the Sulchyaes. He's got...what? What's wrong? Why are you looking at me that way?"

The nurse eyed Mierta, noticing the colour of his robe was no longer its royal blue. "Your entire robe is covered in blood."

"Yes," Mierta answered solemnly before removing his robe and setting it on the ground. "Lochlann has lost a tremendous amount of blood, but that's okay. It will help rid his body of the wound infection currently plaguing him." Mierta's face suddenly went pale and he found himself collapsing into a nearby chair as the gravity of the situation hit him. His eyes filled with tears. "I did what I could in the forest to treat him, but I fear it wasn't enough. He'll die if I can't stop the bleeding."

"And that you will!" the nurse encouraged. "You are the son of our kingdom's court physician. I have seen you work with your father, and you most certainly have his talent. Therefore, tell me how I can assist you."

Mierta wiped tears from his face as he refocused his mind, smearing Lochlann's blood from his hands to his face. He stood up and clapped his hands together. "All right. I'll need bandages, hot water, ale, hemlock, grounded willow bark, and as much of an anaesthetic as you can find. Also, a pillow and blankets. I reckon that table is as horribly uncomfortable as it looks."

"Yes, right away."

He reached out and grabbed the arm of the nurse before she took off to gather the things he had requested, startling her.

"Sorry. I forgot thread. I need as much thread as you can get your hands on."

"Of course," she said, observing the blood that now had been smeared onto her sleeve. "I'll bring warm water and clean towels for you to wash up with as well."

Mierta looked down at his hands. "Yes, that would be wise. Thank you."

He waited until the nurse had left the room before he rolled up the sleeves of his shirt. Leaning into the table, he spoke to the air, purposefully not looking directly at Lochlann's bloodied face. "Now, you listen here, little brother. You aren't going to die. I won't allow it! You just had to wander off and get yourself hurt didn't ya? Can't leave you alone for a minute, can I? Gods! You are such an idiot!" Mierta said in frustration.

Whether or not Lochlann heard, Mierta could not tell, but at the moment he really didn't care.

"I can't risk you waking up while I'm fixing you, so I'm going to cast a spell to help you take a long nap," he said, reaching into his pocket for his wand, pointing it at Lochlann's head. "*Doltedormira.*"

COINNEACH CASTLE—
THE KINGDOM OF VANDOLAY
1248 CE

THE SOUND of mead being poured into a cup filled the room. Mortain handed it over to Déor.

"Your mead, Your Grace."

"Thank you, Mortain," the king answered, taking in the delightful smells. "May I inquire what's in it?"

"Why, it is your favourite mead, Your Grace. Can you not tell by its flavour?"

Déor took a small sip, tasting the gorse flower dry mead that finished with the sweet taste of honey, coconut, and vanilla as they gently travelled down his throat. He also detected something else that was well diluted in it. "Of course I can, court physician. You think I would not recognise the late king's favourite mead? I was merely inquiring if you added anything extra, like something that is carrot-like?"

Mortain bit his lip, trying not to laugh. "That would be hemlock, Your Grace. It will help you sleep."

"Very well," Déor said, taking a larger sip before placing the cup down on a nightstand. "You must be dreadfully worried about your son. Please, know I will do what I can to help locate him, and in the meantime I will pray for his safe return."

"I thank you for your kind words, Your Grace," Mortain answered, though it was impossible to hide his worried expression.

"I am confident Mierta and Orlynd will succeed," Déor said, laying a hand over Mortain's right shoulder.

"We found him, Yir Grace!" Orlynd said with urgency, startling everyone as he abruptly entered the room followed by a frustrated Thomas.

"Oh, thank the good Lord!" Mortain said.

"Orlynd O'Brien, Your Grace," Thomas said after Orlynd had already entered without permission.

Déor raised his hand to acknowledge his guard. "Thank you, Thomas. You may leave us. And, please see to it that no one else enters unannounced?"

"Aye, Your Grace," Thomas said, bowing and promptly leaving the room.

"Orlynd, I want to hear a full report. Tell us everything. I assume you bring us good news?" the king said. Observing the look on Orlynd's face, however, he changed his own expression to a look of concern and said, "Or am I mistaken?"

Worry filled Mortain's face.

Orlynd sighed. "Ah'm afraid Ah come bearing solemn news, Yir Grace. We found Lochlann in Cara Forest. He hud been grievously injured, most likely by the Sulchyaes. Mierta has taken him tae the sanatorium fir treatment. We dinnae know…"

Before Orlynd could say anything further, Mortain was running out of the king's private apartment.

A worried Thomas peered in the open door and caught the king's eye.

"Let him go, Thomas."

"Aye, Your Grace." Thomas bowed and silently closed the door.

The king turned back to Orlynd. "Now, explain how you came to find Lochlann so grievously injured."

COINNEACH CASTLE—
THE KINGDOM OF VANDOLAY
1248 CE

MORTAIN QUICKLY opened the door to the sanatorium and froze in his steps. Everything was eerily quiet; not a sound met his ears except for the creak of the door. It was as if everyone was being secretive on purpose, like they were waiting for the apocalypse.

Looking around he saw a group of people gathered around a table toward the back of the room. He spotted Mierta easily as he was the tallest one there, and the only one working with thread. Then he noticed Mierta was wearing an apothecary sash on top of his normal attire, which contained many remedies and tools that could be used at any occasion. He appeared to be performing some kind of medical procedure. It was difficult to tell what Mierta was doing because of the crowd that surrounded the table.

"Lochlann?" Mortain whispered in surprise.

Mierta, having only finished the last suture, looked up and saw his father standing near the doorway. He didn't want his father to see Lochlann, not like this. Mierta set down the bone needle and promptly walked over to Mortain.

"Mierta," Mortain said, noticing the blood over his son's attire. "Oh, my dear Lord. How is he?"

"I won't lie." Mierta gazed at his father as he carefully chose his words before answering. "It's grim, but there's no need to panic. Not yet, anyway. He's still alive."

"What happened?" Mortain asked, shocked.

"What happened?" Mierta said. "We found him in Cara Forest. He'd been attacked by the Sulchyaes and left for dead, no doubt about that. His injuries are identical to others we've been treating. I've successfully treated and closed most of the wounds, but I still need time to finish the rest."

"Allow me to assist you," Mortain said.

Mierta crinkled his brow and looked down. "I reckon it would be better if you didn't."

"Do not be ridiculous," Mortain said. "I am the court physician. It is my duty to provide healing regardless of who the patient is. Do not forget it was I who had to treat you when you nearly died from the *Acidum Salis!*"

"I haven't forgotten," Mierta said with a pained face, lifting his hand to touch his left cheek where the scar from that time remained.

"Then we shall talk no more of this. Show me Lochlann."

Mierta turned, sighed and promptly brought his father over to the table they were using now as a surgical table.

Lochlann lay on his back with a small pillow under his head. His face was white with the loss of blood and his eyes were sunken into his skull. His body was exposed so they could work on him. Several long wounds covered his chest, abdomen, and arms. Most had been sutured closed but were red and had angry welts along them. The contrast between them and his pale skin was shocking to look at. The wounds that hadn't been sutured still seeped bloody fluid.

"What did you use to slow the bleeding?"

"Wine."

Mortain reacted with surprise. "Good thinking, my boy." He looked up at one of the nurses standing around. "Hand me the bandages and antiseptic. Mierta, you finish the suturing."

"Yes, Father," Mierta said as he went back to working on his brother.

After he had finished suturing the last wound closed, he looked angrily at his father, thinking if only he had been permitted to look for Lochlann when he had requested, circumstances may have been altered.

CHAPTER THIRTEEN

COINNEACH CASTLE—
THE KINGDOM OF VANDOLAY
1248 CE

T he next morning, Mierta opened his eyes in the upstairs bedroom of the small apothecary his father had been given by the king. He sat up off the rough straw mattress and rubbed his aching back, realising it wasn't the most comfortable of beds. He then stared at Lochlann's empty, unmade bed.

Don't worry, Lochlann. You'll be better soon. I can't wait for you to open your eyes so I can tell you that we can go back home and spar! You'll see. I promise.

Mierta's facial expression switched to one of anger. That would only happen if the attacks stopped and the Sulchyaes was captured, or better yet, killed. He reached under the bed for his satchel then stood up and headed down the warped wooden staircase.

When he reached the bottom, he froze. Mierta's eyes widened in shock. The usually tidy room was in shambles. Papers and books were strewn over every flat surface and some were on the floor. The basket that once contained fruit was tilted haphazardly on one of the chairs, and a mug with some sort of liquid had been knocked over and spilled onto the floor. Mierta grabbed his wand from the pocket of his breeches, preparing for a fight, thinking someone had been rummaging through the room looking for valuables. He carefully surveyed the room but saw no one.

"Father," Mierta said, worry on his face.

Quickly, he placed his wand back in his pocket and raced to the sanatorium. When he opened the door, he was met with a brand-new horror. His father was standing over Lochlann, who had gotten worse in the night after he had been moved him from the table to a cot.

"Hold on, Lochlann!" Mortain exclaimed, watching his son's body stiffen. He turned his attention to a nurse. "The fever's gotten worse. Hold his feet still. He's having a fit!"

Lochlann's body began to jerk uncontrollably. Mierta watched helplessly as Mortain threw himself across Lochlann's chest, as Lochlann's arms pushed out and flopped at the sides of the cot. His legs bent and straightened at irregular intervals and his head banged against the pillow. Despite their best efforts, Mortain and the nurse were barely able to keep Lochlann from falling off the cot.

"Lochlann," Mierta whispered. His eyes widened when the fit ended and he caught a glimpse of how red and irritated the wounds he had sutured the previous day now appeared.

He watched as Mortain carefully laid a finger over his brother's neck where the pulse would be felt.

After letting out a deep breath, Mortain paused before speaking again. "His heart momentarily stopped. That fit almost took him. I can't risk him having another one. I need leeches brought to me immediately."

"Yes, sir," the nurse said.

"Lochlann, no," Mierta whispered again as tears of anger began to run down the front of his face. He strode over to a nearby table and slammed his fists down upon it.

The abrupt sound drew everyone's attention and alerted them that Mierta had at some point entered the room.

"Mierta?" Mortain said. He watched as Mierta angrily grabbed the edges of his cloak and turned to walk toward the door of the sanatorium.

"Mierta? Mierta, where are you going?" Mortain called.

"For a walk!" Mierta shouted back. Then he muttered under his breath before slamming the door behind him. "To see Master Ezekiel."

KAVANAGH APOTHECARY— THE KINGDOM OF VANDOLAY 1248 CE

BY THE time Mierta reached his master's apothecary in the kingdom of Vandolay, he had calmed down a bit. The apothecary was in a small building tucked away between two larger ones. It had two windows that covered the front and were divided by a door. The sign that hung on the front of the building said Kavanagh Apothecary and had a pestle and mortar on it with small vials pictured as well. The wood of the building had been whitewashed to make it stand out amongst the other buildings around it.

Mierta sighed as he searched his pockets and robe for the key to the apothecary, unable to locate it.

"Crikey! Must have left the key on the table in the cellar back at home. I'll never hear the end of it from Master Ezekiel." He reached into his pocket again and retrieved his wand. "Hopefully he's in the back mixing some potion and not standing at the counter so I can avoid this embarrassment. He always seems to know whenever I use magic."

Mierta held his right arm out and pointed his wand at the door to the front entrance.

"*Obrate foriando!*"

The sound of a lock unbolting met his ears. He grabbed a hold of the handle, turned it and pushed the door open. The inside of the apothecary was entirely made of wood. There was a single counter near the back where most of the transactions were carried out. The three walls were covered floor to ceiling with shelves containing drawers. The drawers had different ingredients for making potions and poultices.

"Mierta, I wasn't expecting you," Ezekiel Kavanagh said, not looking up from the manuscript he was reading directly behind the counter.

"Master Ezekiel," Mierta said, feeling heat coming to his cheeks. *How does he always know it's me?*

"Should I suggest turning your pinkie finger into a key?" he said sarcastically.

Ezekiel was an attractive man with fair skin and long, dark brown hair. He carried himself with an air of self-importance, with his head held high. Once, he had served as a professor for the University of Noramptone in Edesia before he chose to return and open an apothecary in the kingdom of Vandolay. It was at Coinneach Castle where Ezekiel had first encountered Mierta, after the boy and Mortain had been summoned to the castle to help with Orlynd's illness. He had been so impressed with Mierta's knowledge of poisons that he decided to offer Mierta an apprenticeship.

While inside the shop, he wore a dark blue cap on his head to hold back his hair. The cap also covered his ears and fastened under his chin. He had a sleeveless dark blue robe that was unfastened at the front over a long-sleeved white shirt. The shirt was tied at the neck and was adorned with necklaces of crystals, shells, and sacred wood.

Mierta crinkled his brow. "No, Master," he said, putting his wand away.

THE RITE OF ABNEGATION

"Well then, what pleasure do I have for this unplanned visit?" Master Ezekiel said, looking up with a grin.

"It's my brother, Lochlann. He's become gravely injured."

Ezekiel raised an eyebrow. "Has he now. I'm sorry to hear that." He continued to read the manuscript, uninterested in what Mierta had said.

Mierta stared at his former master, dumbfounded. "Master Ezekiel, did you not hear what I said?"

"Yes, and what is your purpose in telling me this?"

"Because it's my brother," Mierta said. "He was attacked by the Sulchyaes in Cara Forest. I did everything you taught me to treat wound fever. I sutured the wounds, I cleaned them with antiseptic, and yet he continues to worsen. I do not understand."

Master Ezekiel continued to read his manuscript, which irritated Mierta further.

"Would you look at me!"

Master Ezekiel carefully laid the manuscript down on the counter and looked Mierta in the face. "Your father is the court physician. I have taught you everything there is to know about apothecary. You could have been a Master with your own apothecary yourself if you had only taken the exam, but you chose not. You know that if these two things cannot combine to save your brother's life, then perhaps you should be talking to a vicar to prepare his transition."

"No!" Mierta yelled as one of the nearby potion vials shattered.

Master Ezekiel sighed but remained calm, already aware that Mierta's unusual telekinesis ability galvanised when he became upset. "I'm sorry, Mierta. There's nothing I can do that you haven't already tried. You must accept his fate."

Mierta's eyes filled with tears, unable to believe his master's response. "I thought you could help him. Obviously, you can't."

As Mierta turned to walk away, he heard Ezekiel say, "You still haven't learned how to accept defeat. You can't play God and save everybody. People are going to die!"

"Not on my watch," Mierta said, opening the door and slamming it behind him.

Master Ezekiel shook his head. "Took me four days to make that potion. Oh, by God's breath, why did he have to break that one?"

CHAPTER FOURTEEN

THE KINGDOM OF VANDOLAY
1248 CE

Mierta exited the apothecary of his former master, slamming the door behind him. He promptly pulled the hood of his cloak over his face before he started to walk away. He couldn't believe his master had refused to offer him any kind of assistance. It was cruel, the mere suggestion of needing to speak with a vicar. What could the church do for him? Lend him prayer? Prayer had done nothing to bring back his dead mother, whose killer had not been caught. Therefore, prayer would do nothing to help his brother.

"Excuse me," a rather aggressive male vendor spoke, walking a trolley full of fruits and vegetables. He manoeuvred the trolley so he was deliberately blocking Mierta's path. "Excuse me! If you please, sir."

"Get out of my way!" Mierta said, shoving the trolley, causing the entire thing to tip over.

"Blimey! You didn't have to go and do that now, did ya?" the vendor said, looking at the ruined produce on the ground.

Abruptly, a shriek rang out from above. Mierta instinctively reached for his wand. Looking around he could see people running for whatever cover they could.

"Run for your life. It's the monster!" cried a young woman who nearly knocked Mierta over trying to find a place to hide.

Mierta regained his balance and looked up into the sky in the direction where he could hear the evil screeching sound. He gasped. There was a creature flying in the sky that had the head of a Krampus, a body of a lion, claws of an eagle, wings of a black bird, and the tail of a snake.

"The Sulchyaes," Mierta whispered, whipping down the cloak from around his face.

Oh no you don't. You think you're going to come right in here again and kill another? Well, I've got a surprise for you! Have a taste of my wand!

Mierta chased after the creature until he was in an area where he could take aim. He stopped, pointed his wand into the air in the direction of the Sulchyaes and yelled, *"Diplofilla explotar!"*

A dark, parasitic force of repressed energy manifested and shot out of his wand. It rolled and snaked its way in the air toward the creature. Once it hit the Sulchyaes's left wing, it exploded into a black cloud.

The Sulchyaes let out a pained cry as it flapped its wings and turned to leave the area. Once the creature had disappeared in the distance, a crowd began to gather around a shocked Mierta.

"By the Gods. I can't believe it."

"He hit it!"

"He saved our lives!"

"No, no," Mierta said, not wishing for the extra attention as the crowd continued to gather around him. "I did nothing of the sort."

Mierta stood in a bit of a daze, trying to recall where he had learned that particular spell and how he knew to use it against the monster. All he could remember was finding it written in a book he had come across in the library while exploring the kingdom on a free day during his apprenticeship.

"Very honoured to meet you, Mr. Warlock," an elderly man said, shaking Mierta's hand over and over again, bringing him back to the present.

He observed a much larger group of residents had now managed to gather around him. Mierta slowly lifted his head and looked out of the corner of his eye, his mouth in a slight frown.

"You, sir, are a hero!"

Yeah. Sure!

Shortly after, two members of the king's soldiers approached the crowd to break it up. "What's the meaning of this? Go on along your ways."

Once the crowd had vanished, one of the guards looked at Mierta. "Are you the warlock who cast that spell that hurt the Sulchyaes?" he asked matter-of-factly.

Mierta crossed his arms. "I am. Why? Who wants to know?"

"No one has ever been able to injure that monster. His Majesty must be informed of this good news right away. You must come with us immediately!"

Mierta shook his head. "Sorry. That will not be possible. I must return to the sanitorium to help my father with the injured. My duty is there."

The guards immediately grabbed Mierta and proceeded to drag him toward the castle and the great hall.

"We must insist the king hear about this great feat of yours!"

"You don't understand," Mierta said, trying unsuccessfully to fight them off. "I'm the court physician's son! Get your hands off me! I demand you release me at once!"

COINNEACH CASTLE—
THE KINGDOM OF VANDOLAY
1248 CE

"AND LAST, Your Majesty," the Edesia ambassador said, seated at the opposite end of the large dining table in the king's private apartment. "Edesia has denied your request for aid against the monster."

Orlynd, seated to the right of the king, sat in silence as Déor took his time finishing his cup of mead before setting it on the table.

"Thank you, ambassador. It is disappointing to learn of this news, but not surprising. Their king has been after my throne since my father was king. Alas, they would rather watch the destruction of my kingdom from the inside so they can simply come in and take it when I am at my weakest."

"Your Grace?" the ambassador questioned, looking for clarification to his statement.

"May I suggest persuading the king of Edesia to reconsider my request? His ill regard shall not be forgotten. He would not be pleased if I should start taxing his suppliers."

"Of course, Your Majesty," the ambassador said, a bit uneased.

A commotion of loud voices coming from the main room of the king's private apartment caught their attention.

"Did you lot not hear me before? I am required in the sanatorium to assist my father, the court physician!" Mierta protested.

"Thit's Mierta, Yir Grace," Orlynd acknowledged, recognising his voice.

Déor stood from his chair and addressed the ambassador. "Let us hope our next audience brings good news. You may see yourself off now. There is another urgent matter I must attend to."

"Yes, Your Majesty," the ambassador said, standing up from his chair. He bowed before he took his leave.

Déor turned to his soothsayer. "Orlynd, with me."

The king and his soothsayer approached the main area of the king's private apartment where they were met by Mierta and two of the king's guards.

"Thomas, may I inquire why it was necessary to interrupt my meeting with the Edesia ambassador with your racket?"

"I'm so sorry, Your Grace," Thomas said, bowing. "I normally would not intrude; however, the kingdom was only now under attack by the Sulchyaes."

"Again? Now?" Déor said, perplexed. "Why did the bells of Tower Chainnigh not send out a warning? I want all soldiers capable of protecting this kingdom at their posts immediately!" He reached for his sword. "And why in God's breath did you take Mierta away from his duties? He is not part of this."

"That's what I tried to tell them," Mierta said matter-of-factly. *Honestly, they probably wouldn't have listened to me anyway.*

"But he is, sire!" the other guard said. "Swords won't be necessary. The Sulchyaes has already flown away thanks to this warlock's magic spell."

"What?" Déor said, turning to Mierta.

"I couldn't believe it at first either, Your Grace, but it's true. He damaged the creature," Thomas said.

"How? Our weapons have been useless."

"*Diplofilla explotar,*" Mierta said, looking down with a frown. "I reckon it's black magic."

"Orlynd," Déor said, turning back to his soothsayer. "Can you confirm?"

"Nay, Yir Grace," Orlynd said. "Ah'm unfamiliar wi black magic spells; however, thit encyclopaedia Ah read did indicate black magic wis the way ay harming it."

"This is fantastic news, a cause for a celebration! Let all of the kingdom know we have discovered the enemy's weakness."

"Yes, Your Grace," Thomas said, turning to leave.

"Your Grace, may I be permitted to return to my duties? My brother, I'm afraid, has become further ill. I must get back to helping my father tend to him and the others still sick and injured."

"Of course," Déor said.

Mierta bowed and turned toward the door. "One more thing. May I also have a moment alone with your soothsayer? There's something rather important I must discuss with him."

"By all means." Déor gestured to Orlynd to follow Mierta.

COINNEACH CASTLE— THE KINGDOM OF VANDOLAY 1248 CE

ORLYND AND Mierta walked down a long hallway that ran the length of Coinneach Castle. The walls were stained a dark red and the flooring was made of cherrywood. As they walked down this hallway, Orlynd couldn't help but feel a bit uncomfortable, especially because whenever he walked down this hall, it was like the eyes of the ancestors of the royal family were watching him due to all of the various portraits. If it weren't for the many strategically placed windows, the hall would have been in complete darkness.

They had turned down another hall when Mierta abruptly pushed Orlynd into the wall.

"Tell me my brother is going to recover," Mierta said, pointing a finger at him in a threatening way.

"Ah dinnae understand whit yis r going oan about," Orlynd said.

Mierta revealed his wand from his pocket. "You have the gift of foresight. I've seen you do it. Tell me my brother has a future!"

Orlynd opened his mouth to speak while raising his hands. "Listen tae me. Ah know yis r upset. If it wis ma brother, Ah wid be, tae. But yis must understand. Ma gift, it dinnae work like thit."

"Don't lie to me!" Mierta said, tears filling his eyes.

"Ah'm sorry. Ah cannae control whit oar when Ah can see. Ah can only pray thit he'll recover."

Mierta let go of Orlynd, defeated, and put his wand away.

Orlynd raised an eyebrow. "He's nae?"

Mierta nodded his head but then shook it. "No, not yet. But he's getting worse, Orlynd. My treatment…it's failing. I don't know what to do. He's fading and I am helpless to stop it. Even Master Ezekiel refused to help."

Then a thought crossed Orlynd's mind. The story he remembered enjoying the most from the encyclopaedia was about the Aos Sí, a group of people lost to legend. What if they weren't merely a legend?

"Thir may be someone, but thir's nae any guarantee," Orlynd started.

"What? Tell me who it is and where I can find them?" Mierta said urgently.

"They r called the Aos Sí. They r the guardians ay the lakes ay Iverna and Lorrina. They were the first race tae settle in Iverna but were driven away tae live underground. Most ay them moved tae an island west ay Iverna called Koconea, except thit island cannae exist because it's never been found."

"Yes, I've heard of them. Father would say the reason humans have skill in swordsmanship is due to their teachings," Mierta said.

"Aye. N Ah'm reckoning they r still here in Iverna. If yis bring them an offer ay milk n butter, they may be able tae give yis a remedy tae help save yir brother."

"But how am I to find them? There haven't been any reports of them in ages. It is hopeless."

"Nay!" Orlynd said. "It's nae hopeless. Yis can find them. Ah believe if anyone can it is yis. Think, where is someplace thit is near water n is underground?"

Mierta thought for several moments before blurting out, "The mermaid cavern! It's located directly underneath Castle Tarloch. No one would ever go there because the castle's staff is always preoccupied with keeping up with all of its prisoners. Blimey! Orlynd, you are brilliant! I cannot thank you enough. I must be off. It will take me two days to get there by carriage. Please, look after my father and brother while I'm gone, and if the Sulchyaes should dare to return, remember *diplofilla explotar*."

CHAPTER FIFTEEN

THE MERMAID CAVERN—
GLENDALOW
1248 CE

The entrance to the mermaid cavern was surrounded by rocks and covered by sea grasses. It contained a low-ceilinged opening that had been cut by the rough waters of the lake. The rock walls were wet and rough-hewn with bits of the same sea grass hanging precariously from fissures in the rock. The tinkle of water dripping onto the rocks echoed through the cavern.

The sound of Mierta's feet stepping on wet sea stones of various sizes, which covered the floor of the cavern, reverberated as he traversed the cavern.

"Um, hello? Is anyone there?" he spoke, hopping onto the next sea stone.

The passageway inside could barely be seen as no sunlight could penetrate beyond the opening. Instinctively, Mierta reached into his pocket for his wand.

"*Scamos lias!*" Mierta chanted as a dim, turquoise, florescent light sparkled from the tip of his wand.

He raised it in front of him, noticing the ceiling had opened up enough to enable him to stand and look around. There were several different passageways leading off the main chamber, which could cause one to become lost if one were careless.

Doesn't look like anyone's been here in a long time.

He turned and frowned, noticing the tide had come in slightly farther than he had. *Great, I reckon I'm going to have to be wary of the time. The high tide would likely trap me on the inside and perhaps even drown me.*

"Who is there?" said what sounded like a grumpy old man, coming from one of the passageways.

Mierta gasped and quickly regained his composure. He clapped his hands and rubbed them together.

"Ah! Yes. Hello. I'm looking for someone. They go by the name of the Aos Sí. Do you know where I may be able to find them?"

"Perhaps," said the voice of its owner, remaining out of sight. The man continued up the passageway. "But my questions require answers first. Who are you? Tell me why you are here."

"My name's Mierta. Mierta McKinnon."

"McKinnon," he said, acknowledging. "A very strong family name. Go on."

"I've come to seek aid for my brother. He is ill."

"How?"

"He was attacked by a creature conceived by using black magic called the Sulchyaes."

"And why should I help you?" he said as he continued to listen.

"Because his life doesn't deserve to end this way. He only had his twelfth birthday and he succeeded in his Rite of Wands ceremony." Mierta could now see a form of a person standing in the shadow. His heart began to race as tears filled his eyes. "Please. If you truly are the Aos Sí. Help me. Help me believe that our futures can be changed!"

An older man with wild silver-grey hair then slipped out of the shadow while Mierta continued to speak, looking toward the ground.

"I bring an offering! Milk and butter in exchange for my brother's restored health."

Mierta pulled the satchel from around his cloak and set it down on the ground. Squatting, he went through the bag until he found the items Orlynd had suggested he bring for an offering. He placed them in front of him. Then, he looked up and gasped.

Standing before him was an old man wearing a light cloak that had many different colours in it. His silver-grey hair stood out from his head and his eyes were glowing with a blue light. There was also a white, shimmering glow surrounding his body, hindering the necessity for the light from Mierta's wand.

Mierta stood up, shook the light out of his wand, put it away, and allowed his eyes to adjust. "Your form…it's very alluring. Who are you? Are you the Aos Sí?"

"I have many different names. Some call me the Aos Sí, Daoine Sídhe, the Shining Folk, the Gentry, the Good Neighbours. But you may call me Caeilte. I am king of what remains of the Tuatha Dé Danann tribe. I am a representation of what it means to be kind."

"Kind? So, that means you will help me?" Mierta said, wiping the tears from his face.

"Yes, Mierta McKinnon," Caeilte said, grinning and raising his eyebrows. "I will help you save your brother."

Caeilte promptly removed his cloak, revealing a green garment of some kind of soft material underneath that had braided gold ribbons running from shoulder to foot as it fell to the ground. There was also a heavy leather belt cinched around his waist.

He's wearing that *under that cloak? He may as well be wearing two cloaks! Blimey! Never seen anything so preposterous.*

Then, Mierta noticed a leather gauntlet with three vials on his right arm, filled with glowing liquid the same colour as Caeilte's eyes.

"What is that?" he asked, watching Caeilte lift one of the vials.

"Alshtatten." Caeilte smiled, bringing the vial out toward Mierta. "I use it to sustain me."

"Hang on," Mierta said. "Correct me if I'm wrong. You are immortal, are you not? You would have no use for sustenance. Why would you even carry the Alshtatten other than for some kind of entitlement?"

"Is that what you really think, warlock?" Caeilte said, feeling insulted. "You would be wise not to make me angry. I may take back my offer to help you."

"No, no, please. I'm sorry. I didn't mean to offend."

Caeilte continued, "The Aos Sí is composed of two beings— male and female. My wife, the queen, is immortal. However, I am not. I am getting old and withered. Yes, by the look on your face, what you're thinking is correct. This body is dying. Once the Alshtatten runs out, I too shall perish and go back into the ground as ashes and dust."

"And those three vials are all you have left?" Mierta asked, crinkling his brow.

"Enough to sustain me for three more lifetimes," Caeilte said with a smile. "And now, two." Caeilte then tried to hand the vial to Mierta.

"I do not understand," Mierta said, hesitating to take the vial.

"Your brother must consume its entire contents. Then, and only then, it will restore his health. Here, take it, before I change my mind!"

Mierta took the vial and placed it into his satchel. "I don't know how to thank you for your generosity."

Caeilte smiled with his lips and laughed half-heartedly. "I require no thanks."

Mierta quickly glanced behind him, realising the tide was continuing to come in.

"I should be taking my leave now. The journey to the kingdom of Vandolay is a two-day journey by carriage. I'm honestly not sure if my brother has that much time left to wait."

"Yes," Caeilte acknowledged. "Best to be off then."

Mierta started to turn and stopped abruptly when he heard Caeilte say, "Mierta, don't give up. You are getting closer to compounding a cure."

Mierta swallowed hard and slowly turned back around. "You know about the Shreya? Then, if I'm getting closer, then you must know how to stop it."

"No. I only know it's already been here before. But this time, it's adapted, it's learned, it's become stronger. Heed my warning and heed it well. Many people are going to die before it's all over, including your loved ones if you aren't careful."

"That won't happen. I promise. Thank you again for helping me save Lochlann."

"Yes, well, the debt has already been paid. Off you go to the kingdom of Vandolay. Take care, warlock, and good luck."

Mierta smiled, nodded, and took off running toward the entrance of the cavern.

Once Mierta was gone, Caeilte laughed. "As I said, the debt has already been paid, Mierta. You will bring about your brother's undoing."

Caeilte grinned as he snapped his fingers—as if by doing so, he set the course for an alternate future in motion.

COINNEACH CASTLE—
THE KINGDOM OF VANDOLAY
1248 CE

ORLYND STOOD and stared at the door to the castle's sanatorium, preparing himself for the worst. Mierta had still not returned from the Aos Sí with a remedy, and Lochlann's health was continuing to decline. He opened the door only enough to peek inside, confirming Mortain was still sitting beside Lochlann's sickbed keeping vigil. He sighed deeply before pushing the door open farther. He entered the room quietly and closed it behind him.

As he slowly approached Lochlann's sickbed, he took in the surroundings, seeing things hadn't changed much. The room was still sparsely furnished. There were still six cots in the room arranged along the outside walls with simple mattresses placed between them all. Each bed and mattress held an injured or sick soldier. Simple small tables had been set up in the centre of the room to keep bowls of water and remedies close at hand. The stone walls were devoid of any decoration save for a simple cross above the door. At the far end of the room stood a large wardrobe, which contained clean linens, bandages, and simple potions for the more common ailments. Its doors hung open and bandages hung haphazardly off the shelves.

Once Orlynd had arrived at Lochlann's bed, he stared down at him. He observed Lochlann's chest rise and fall at an abnormally fast pace. Between gasps, it sounded as if his lungs were being constricted by something like fluid, preventing him from taking a proper breath. The largest wounds on his chest were still sutured shut, and smaller wounds were currently being treated with leeches where a mix of blood and pus could be seen seeping out from under them. His face had also gone from pale to a grey-and-purplish skin tone since the last time Orlynd recalled seeing him. Dread filled his heart.

Mierta, where r yis? Orlynd thought to himself, his eyes filling with worry, wondering what could be delaying him. *Yir brother dinnae huv much time.*

"Orlynd," Mortain said, suddenly looking up. "I'm surprised to see you back again so soon."

"Aye. Ah cannae explain it. It feels like Ah'm supposed tae be here, like Ah wid be missing something important if Ah'm nae."

Mortain smiled.

"How is he?" Orlynd said.

Orlynd patiently watched Mortain lift Lochlann's right hand and briefly take it into his, checking his pulse. Then, he carefully laid Lochlann's hand back on the table.

Mortain answered sadly, "The breath is leaving him. His respiratory system is becoming paralysed. Despite all Mierta and I have tried to rid Lochlann of the infection, it continues to take him. Even the leeches cannot get rid of it. Oh, my dear Lord, he's fading." He looked up into Orlynd's face, tears in his eyes. "My son will be gone by nightfall."

"Nay," Orlynd said, trying his best to convince himself otherwise, though doubt had already started to fill his own mind. However, what was important at this moment was convincing Mortain that Lochlann still had a chance of survival. "Yis must hear me oat. Mierta will find the Aos Sí n bring back the medicine necessary tae save Lochlann's life. Yis must nae lose hope."

"Hope? Hope is all I have left. I know the chances of Lochlann's survival are grim. His injuries were already far too grave when you lot brought him here. Even if Mierta would arrive now, I am uncertain… oh, my dear Lord. Where is Mierta? What is taking him so long?"

"He'll be here. Yis know him. He wid never forgive himself if he wid be tae late," Orlynd stated.

"You're right, Orlynd. Mierta is a McKinnon after all, and there's one thing McKinnon's don't do, and that's give up." Mortain smiled slightly as a tear rolled down his cheek. "The two of them are so different, yet Lochlann admires his older brother and would do anything to help him. Did you know when Mierta was the same age as Lochlann, he almost died?"

"Nay," Orlynd said.

"Ah. Yes, I suppose you wouldn't have with all the preparations going on for the king's coronation." Mortain sighed. "I gave Mierta access to one of my early compounding books. I had promised him to demonstrate how, but when the time came, I got distracted by other matters. Mierta decided to give one of the recipes in the book a go and the cauldron exploded suddenly, splashing the left side of his face with *Acidum Salis*. That's how he got that scar," Mortain explained, gesturing toward the left side of his face. "The accident nearly cost him his life. After I took him upstairs and my servant assisted me with getting the remnants of the chemicals out of his hair, he stopped breathing. After it started again, his heart was beating so fast I was certain it was going to give out. It was only by the grace of our good Lord that Mierta survived."

"Then, believe thit will happen again n Mierta will arrive wi the remedy tae save him," Orlynd said. He sighed. "Yis must be exhausted. Please, Ah'll stay here so yis can rest. Yis will nae be able tae properly care fir Lochlann if yis cannae take care ay yirself. If anything should change, Ah'll notify yis at once."

"I am truly thankful for your offer, Orlynd. It saddens me you never got the chance to properly be a big brother to your younger brother, Verlyn. I know in my heart," he said, briefly looking back to Lochlann, "you would have been someone he would have looked up to."

"Aye," Orlynd said solemnly, looking to the floor. "Ah suppose maybe he wid huv."

Mortain smiled again, becoming lost in his own thoughts. *It is no coincidence, Orlynd, that you feel the emotional bond to Lochlann. If only I could tell you the truth; he's your brother, not Mierta's. His real name is Verlyn Tiberius O'Brien.*

CHAPTER SIXTEEN

COINNEACH CASTLE—
THE KINGDOM OF VANDOLAY
1248 CE

I've got the medicine!" Mierta announced, bursting through the door to the sanatorium. Everything was eerily quiet; not a sound met his ears except for a few words here and there. *I hope I haven't arrived too late!*

Mortain was standing over Lochlann's bedside, carefully adjusting Lochlann's body from lying on his side to lying on his back. He turned his attention to his son's voice.

Mierta quickly moved over toward Lochlann's sickbed, taking a seat in the chair. He furrowed his brow, alarmed by his brother's changed skin tone since he last saw him four days ago. The skin on his hands had turned to a blotchy colour and there was a blueish tone to Lochlann's face. His breaths had become shallow with a space of five-to-sixty seconds between each breath.

Feeling a hand on his shoulder, Mierta turned back to his father. "Has Lochlann awoken since I left?"

Mortain shook his head as he removed his hand and patted Mierta on the back for comfort.

"Where's Orlynd?" Mierta asked, noticing the soothsayer wasn't present in the room.

"I made him go home and rest. He's been with your brother non-stop since you left."

"Blimey!" Mierta said. "I will have to give him my thanks a bit later." Then he reached into his satchel and pulled out a small vial containing a glowing blue liquid. As he gazed at the Alshtatten, he looked up at his father. "Reckon he can hear me?"

"Yes, my boy," Mortain answered.

Mierta nodded, sitting down on the edge of Lochlann's sickbed. He positioned his arm gently under his brother's head, feeling the intense heat coming off his body as he propped him up slightly, so he'd be able to consume the mixture. "Okay." He sighed. "Lochlann, listen to me. I am going to pour some draught into your mouth. I know you're incredibly weak, but this will make you better, I promise. I need you to give me all you've got and drink it until it's fully gone." He looked back at his father for reassurance, watching him nod.

"Right." Cautiously, Mierta poured a small amount of the liquid into Lochlann's mouth, observing him for any movement. "Come on, Lochlann." He watched intently until he saw the telltale signs of swallowing. "Yes! That's it! Only a little bit more."

He smiled and continued to pour the contents of the vial until all had been fully consumed. When he was finished, Mierta carefully repositioned Lochlann's head back against his pillow. That's when Mierta heard what sounded like a small cry from his brother.

"Lochlann?" Mierta questioned, his eyes growing wide. He noticed his brother's body had suddenly gone stiff. With panic in his voice, he said, "He's…he's having another fit!"

"Throw yourself over him, my son!"

Obeying, tears began to fill Mierta's eyes as he was unable to believe what was happening. He could feel Lochlann's heart beating uncontrollably as his brother's arms pushed out and flopped at the sides of the cot. Like the one he had witnessed before he left, Lochlann's legs bent and straightened at irregular intervals and his head banged against the pillow. Then everything abruptly stopped. That was when Mierta noticed his brother's chest had suddenly gone still.

"No, no...don't do this to me. You were supposed to get better from the Alshtatten."

"Mierta?" Mortain said, his voice full of worry.

Mierta leaned in, observing that Lochlann's jaw was relaxed and his mouth was partially open. He swiped his hand in front of his brother's face, confirming no air was moving. He also noticed his brother's eyes were fixed, slightly opened, and his pupils were enlarged.

"He's not breathing," he said softly to himself as if he was trying to convince himself of the situation. "Why isn't he breathing?"

Quickly, he placed his ear over the centre of Lochlann's chest, unable to hear a heartbeat. "No, no, no. This cannot be possible."

"Mierta, what's wrong?"

"His heart isn't beating. Lochlann's dead. But he can't be! He can't be!" he muttered to himself before enunciating. "Caeilte promised." He reached a finger up toward the side of Lochlann's neck, placing it there to confirm his brother's heart had given out. Slowly, he looked up at his father, his brow furrowing. "Lochlann's...gone," he stammered, his eyes looking toward the ground, guilt written all over his face. "I'm sorry. The fit took him. Caeilte lied to me."

"What?"

"Father, Lochlann's dead. His heart stopped. I felt it. I'm sorry. I took too long getting the remedy," Mierta said softly as his heart broke. "I've failed you. I've failed you both."

Mortain frowned, comprehending. He walked over to Mierta and placed a hand on the back of his shoulder. "It's not your fault. You did your best, Son. Please, do not blame yourself. Lochlann's body was simply too frail," Mortain said, holding back a sob. "Very few have survived an attack by the Sulchyaes. It was foolish to believe Lochlann would."

"But the Aos Sí promised!" Mierta said, slamming his fist down on the sickbed. "He said the Alshtatten would save Lochlann. Why would he lie to me?"

"Mierta. What are you squawking about?" a weak voice uttered.

Lochlann? Mierta questioned to himself, looking down.

Suddenly, Lochlann gasped, startling both Mierta and Mortain, as new life began to fill the insides of his body.

"Lochlann," Mierta uttered between breaths. "You're…you're alive." *Only, it can't be true. It's impossible. I verified myself. He was dead.*

Lochlann eyed his brother with confusion. "Of course I am, Mierta. What are you going on about?" Lochlann moaned in pain as his wounds were still very serious.

"Alshtatten," Caeilte had said. "I use it to sustain me."

The Alshtatten. The Alshtatten is an elixir of life. Lochlann really did die, but the elixir brought him back, renewed. Lochlann died! He was supposed to die, but I changed his future! Blimey! There's no determining what consequences my actions may bring.

Mierta watched with awe as his brother's skin tone returned to a healthy colour.

"Nothing to worry yourself about, Lochlann." Mortain stepped up to Lochlann's bedside, barely able to contain his joy. "I'm sure Mierta is merely a bit overwhelmed at the moment and very relieved to see you awake," Mortain added, placing a hand over Mierta's shoulder again, practically startling Mierta back to the present. "You have been very ill, and he and I have been looking after you."

"Where am I? How long have I been here?" Lochlann asked, glancing around the room.

"You are in the sanatorium of Coinneach Castle. You were attacked by the Sulchyaes and you've been asleep for five days," Mortain said. "We nearly lost you."

"Blimey!" Lochlann said as he relaxed back against the pillow, once again moaning against the pain of his wounds. He began to see flashes of the attack, the creature and the man who was controlling it. "Mierta," he whined.

"Hey," Mierta whispered, crinkling his brow. "It's all right. I'm here. We'll give you something to help with the pain."

Lochlann nodded.

Mierta stood up from the sickbed and proceeded to search through his satchel. He pulled out a different vial of liquid.

"Here," Mierta said, putting his arm under Lochlann's head again in order to support him. "It will make you sleepy, but that's okay. You'll need rest to further regain your strength."

He watched Lochlann drink down the concoction before he took the empty vial away. Then, he helped Lochlann lay back down on the cot.

"Mierta, I have to tell you something," Lochlann said.

Mierta readjusted the chair. "Yes? What is it?"

"There was a warlock in Cara Forest who could control the Sulchyaes. His name was Tarik. Before he set that creature on me, he told me to inform you he desired to have a duel with you."

"A warlock duel? Is that so? Well," Mierta said, standing up from the chair, "if a duel is what he wishes for, then he will have it! Tell me how to contact him."

CHAPTER SEVENTEEN

COINNEACH CASTLE—
THE KINGDOM OF VANDOLAY
1248 CE

"Son, you don't have to do this," Mortain said, watching Mierta pace around the small apothecary.

Earlier that morning a pigeon had arrived with a message from Tarik responding to Mierta's inquiry about a warlock duel.

"Yes, I do," Mierta said, grabbing an apple out of the fruit basket, taking a bite out of it. He then gathered parchment, a quill and some ink and brought them over to the table before taking a seat. He dipped the quill into the black ink. "Tarik has challenged me to a warlock duel; therefore, I must accept. Otherwise our family's name may be tarnished."

"Never mind about that, Mierta. The reputation of our family name isn't important. It's already been tarnished by mistakes I've made."

Mierta continued as if he hadn't heard what his father had said. He paused to finish composing the letter to Tarik.

"I shall send his pigeon back to him with this message to meet me in Cara Forest this afternoon, along with his creature."

"Mierta," Mortain said with a warning in his voice, watching Mierta put the quill down.

"You don't have to worry about me, Father. I can do this. Trust me. I will succeed," Mierta said, looking up toward him.

"My son, you are not invincible!" He sighed, frustrated, watching Mierta get up from the table and start to finish preparing the letter for the pigeon. "Look, I know you mean well, but listen to me. You will not do anyone any good if you come back dead. I need you here. I can't let you risk forfeiting your life in this way!"

"Father, I won't die there. I know that is not my destiny," Mierta said, sending the pigeon off before looking his father straight in the face. "There's something much more important I'm supposed to do."

"Son, if you're referring to your Rite of Wands, I must caution you! The Rite of Wands ceremony is merely a test of the mind. What it shows you is a piece of what your life may be like. It's not a guarantee. Your life can change. Think of how many times your life has changed simply by how you chose to react to something."

"I don't understand. You reminded me of Lord Kaeto exactly now and the advice he gave me when I was a little boy," Mierta said.

Mortain smiled with his lips and sighed in resignation as he laid his hands on Mierta's shoulders. "Then, listen to me. I know I cannot stop you. The only caution I can give you is this: don't let your arrogance show. I don't want you to be making the same kind of mistakes that I did when I was a young boy. It nearly cost me everything. Be careful and come back alive."

"I will, Father. I promise."

CARA FOREST—
THE KINGDOM OF VANDOLAY
1248 CE

"WELL, WELL, well," Tarik said, watching Mierta walk up the path with his wand in hand.

Mierta noticed it was the same path where he and Orlynd had found Lochlann.

"Colour me impressed. You actually showed. Didn't reckon you would."

Mierta smiled at him smugly. "If there's one thing about me you should know it's that I don't take threats lightly." Mierta noticed the Sulchyaes in the trees behind Tarik.

"Is that so? Say, how's that brother of yours? Dead now, I presume?" Tarik smirked.

"No," Mierta answered with a sneer. "Quite well, actually. He's making a full recovery as we speak, in fact."

Tarik huffed. "Shame. Well then, I guess you'll have to replace him, hmm?" He reached into his pocket and took out his wand.

"Ha!" Mierta laughed. "Forgive me if I don't go down as easily as my brother."

The warlocks positioned their wands at the ready and slowly walked toward each other. As Mierta bowed to his opponent, he was careful to not lose sight of the Sulchyaes. His strategy was to weaken the creature before severely injuring Tarik. However, he had no intention of actually killing the warlock even though he had admitted to himself he was tempted.

Believing his opponent was distracted by the Sulchyaes, Tarik mocked as he bowed to Mierta, "I would be scared of him, too, if I were you. Best to get a good look at him now before he kills you."

The warlocks turned and walked approximately twenty paces away from each other.

As Mierta turned around again, he took in a deep breath before raising his wand toward Tarik. He counted down from three in his head before shouting, "*Diplofilla explotar!*"

A dark, parasitic force of manifested, repressed energy shot out of his wand, rolling and snaking its way in the air toward the Sulchyaes, exploding into a black cloud as it made a direct hit to its chest. The Sulchyaes screamed in pain.

At the same time, Tarik shouted, "*Vorbíllion!*"

Mierta was promptly lifted into the air and thrown a few feet backwards before his back made contact with the ground. "Ooof!" Before he was even able to recover from the fall, Tarik cast *"Palavariso"* and Mierta's wand was lifted out of his hand and thrown into the red leaves lying all over the ground behind him. Mierta's eyes went wide with fright.

I'm so incredibly daft! I should have accounted for the possibility of Tarik using a disarming charm.

Mierta looked up at the Sulchyaes, hearing it growl, as he slowly backed up using his hands and feet, crab-like.

All right, Mierta. Now's not the time to panic!

"Heh." Tarik laughed. "This is when I would suggest you run." He raised his hand and pointed at Mierta. "Sulchyaes, attack!"

The Sulchyaes shrieked as it lifted out of the trees and took after Mierta.

"Ah!" Mierta cried, realising he had no time to call out for his wand. He quickly gained his feet and took off in a run.

"Let me help you with that," Tarik teased, raising his wand. "*Vorbíllion!*"

Mierta was sent flying a few feet ahead of him before he made contact with the ground.

With the surroundings rapidly spinning, Mierta forced himself to focus.

Think, Mierta, think!

He slapped himself on his cheeks multiple times as if it would somehow help the situation.

Stay awake, you fool! If you lose consciousness now, the Sulchyaes will kill you.

He glanced around with blurry vision before his eyes locked on his wand.

I need to get my wand back.

He stood up on shaky legs and concentrated on telepathically calling for his wand. His eyes began to take on the appearance of snake eyes, only when he reached out his right hand, he felt a sharp, stabbing, burning pain down the back of his right shoulder and arm as the claws of the Sulchyaes pierced his skin before it flew back into the air.

"AHH!" Mierta fell to his knees, screaming in agony as he reached out with his left arm and grabbed his right side. "Bad. Very bad. Couldn't see him. Arm...can...hardly...move. Ahhh!" he shrieked into the ground.

He could hear the Sulchyaes screeching in the air above him in between the sound of his own rapid, deep breaths. It wouldn't be much longer before it would decide to dive at him again.

As his vision began to briefly clear, he watched as his own blood started to trickle down the path in front of him before spots quickly replaced his vision and he became physically drained.

This is bad. I'm losing too much blood. I'm going to die here. I underestimated the creature's power.

Mierta stared at his blood blankly until circling, white puffy clouds filled his vision, and he collapsed onto his left side.

There was no knowing how long he had lost consciousness for before a woman's voice startled him awake.

"Mierta!"

Mierta slowly opened his eyes, recognising the voice as belonging to his dear mother. "Mum?" he whispered.

"I'm here, Son," Clarinda said.

Mierta attempted to focus his eyes but was quickly overcome by the vision of a glowing, bright light. As he held his left hand up to shelter his eyes, Mierta abruptly came to the conclusion that his death was imminent, and his brain had already begun the process of accepting his fate by creating this hallucination of being reunited with his beloved mother. Tears filled his eyes. Any moment the Sulchyaes would dive down and deliver his final blow.

"Mother, I'm afraid," he spoke. "I am injured and have lost the use of my right arm."

"Mierta, my boy, your Mum is so proud of you. You have been so brave and have endured so much."

"No, Mum, I have failed. The Sulchyaes is going to kill me. Please…stay. I don't wish to die alone," Mierta said, defeated.

"Mierta, my son, you must not give up now. The Sulchyaes can be defeated."

"I do not know how to, Mum. I'm too weak to defeat it. My life is forfeit."

"No, my boy. You must cast *Petrosani pan war*. That's how you'll rid this world of its evil."

"*Petrosani pan war?*" Mierta uttered. "What's that? Why have I never heard of this spell before?"

Clarinda's voice became more urgent as the light began to fade. "Mierta, time is running out. You must get back up and fight. I love you, Son."

"I love you, too, Mum. Miss you."

"Need some help dying over there, Mierta?" Tarik asked, interrupting Mierta's thoughts, bringing him back to the present. The pain fully raced back to him.

Between cries of pain, Mierta flipped himself onto his back, his head hitting the ground. He clenched his left fist as he waited for his vision to adjust. Then, he cringed as he forced himself to sit back up. The Sulchyaes could be heard in the sky above him, readying itself for the final attack.

"I can't...mustn't...die here."

Groaning in pain, he reached out with his left hand, his eyes taking on the appearance of snake eyes when he shouted, "*Convosuri!*"

The Sulchyaes screeched as it came in for the kill. Its legs were stretched out before it and its talons were spread wide open, ready to rip into Mierta's flesh.

Once Mierta had grabbed a hold of his wand, he crinkled his brow and glanced up at the creature. He had one shot. If he was unsuccessful, then it would all be over...

It was like the world was moving in slow motion. Mierta could hear himself take in slow, deep breaths; his heart was thumping in his chest, and pain stabbed at his side while a piercing ringing filled his ears.

He held his wand out with his left hand again and uttered, "*Petrosani pan war!*" He wasn't sure if he had correctly spoken the spell because to his ears, it sounded like the bellowing of a cow.

Suddenly, the Sulchyaes screeched, pulled up, and with a final flap of his wings, abruptly turned to stone and began breaking apart.

"Blimey! It worked," Mierta said before realising what remained of the Sulchyaes was about to fall right on top of him. "No, no, no!"

He threw himself to the ground, covering his head with his left hand as the Sulchyaes dropped down in front of him, shattering into tiny pieces that showered down on Mierta. "Ah!"

"NO!" Tarik shouted. "That's not possible! How did you do that? How did you do that?! You shouldn't have been able to. He was my creation. I conjured him!"

"*Vorbillion!*" Mierta cast from the ground.

Tarik was hit by the spell and flew backwards, landing on his back hard enough to knock the wind out of his lungs.

"I'm the chosen one," Mierta said with heavy breaths as he stood back up on shaky legs. He pointed his wand at Tarik with a wavering hand. "I'm going to save this land from a much bigger foe than you will ever be. And you know what that is?" He weakly cast the next spell, "*Palavaríso!*"

Tarik's wand was abruptly thrown from his hand.

Mierta stumbled over to Tarik and pointed his wand in the direction of Tarik's heart now that the warlock had been disarmed. He uttered, "It's called the Shreya."

Tarik put his hands up in defeat. He laughed as if mocking Mierta. "What are you going to do, warlock? Kill me? I doubt you have much time left yourself to defeat any Shreya. You're bleeding everywhere!"

"You're right," Mierta confirmed, things becoming hazier. "But I've killed your monster and the people living in the kingdom of Vandolay are safe again. And, once my eyes decide to refocus, I've got something much better planned for you. Don't even think of trying to retrieve your wand. It can't help you this time."

"Halt!" screamed Aindrias and several other king's men. They quickly surrounded Mierta and Tarik.

Tarik laughed again. "Blimey! Where did you lot come from?"

"On orders of the king!" Aindrias said, looking over to Mierta. "Your father informed him you would be out here."

Mierta mouthed a thanks to the king's guard.

"Whoa. Steady there, warlock," Aindrias said, observing Mierta stumble. "You are gravely injured and in need of treatment."

"I'm fine," Mierta lied, feeling suddenly hot and clammy. Nausea was also trying its hardest to build in his throat.

Tarik laughed, bringing everyone's attention back to him. He smirked. "So, what are you all going to do now?"

"We shall assist in escorting you both to the kingdom of Aracelly," Aindrias said. "There, Mierta's wounds will be treated and you will answer for your crimes."

Mierta cut Aindrias short. "You shall be questioned by Dragomir before a small group of warlocks upon which your fate will be decided. Then, you'll answer to Lord Kaeto for what you've done through the Rite of Abnegation!"

"No!" Tarik cried. "You wouldn't do that. Please! I'm a warlock, like you. It's part of who I am."

"I dare you to test me again. You will learn quickly that I am nothing...like...you," Mierta slurred, weakened by the blood loss, watching as the world grew dark. He mumbled something incomprehensible before his knees buckled and he collapsed to the ground.

CHAPTER EIGHTEEN

POVEGLIA—
THE KINGDOM OF ARACELLY
1248 CE

"*Emaculavi el curpas y mehartis.*"

Mierta slowly opened his eyes. He blinked, allowing them to focus. The room was brightly lit by a candle-filled chandelier. The light seemed to bounce off the marble walls. He realized he was laying on a soft bed and several figures were standing around it.

"Where am I?" Mierta said, his voice sounding frightened.

"Hush. You're safe now. Please, don't speak," a woman said, bringing a soothing hand up to lightly touch Mierta's hair, causing him to turn his head in her direction. She looked down into his nervous green eyes before she moved her hand to lay it against his forehead. "My name is Liliana de Caitie. You are in the care now of the healers of Poveglia."

Mierta turned his head, observing the four healers surrounding him, each pointing their wands toward his chest with their right hands while their left hands were lying over his heart. He could see a bright, white light flowing out of the tips of their wands. He became acutely aware that he was not wearing any clothing and he was covered with a simple sheet. He moved to cover himself and realized his arm was heavily bandaged.

Liliana gently put her hand on his arm, forcing it back to the bed, and said, "Do not fear. My staff are working on your healing. You will be all right now." She watched his eyes move back toward her. "It is important you continue to rest. Obey my words."

Mierta could feel his eyes suddenly closing against his will.

DRACONIERA MOUNTAIN— THE KINGDOM OF ARACELLY 1248 CE

TARIK GASPED as the sack made of wolf's hide was lifted from his head. An immediate discomforting light source shined brightly down into his eyes from above. He attempted to shade his eyes; however, he was unable to due to the fact that his wrists were shackled to the armrests of the chair that was located in the centre of a circular chamber.

He couldn't remember much of what had previously happened. He recalled he had been in Cara Forest surrounded by the warlock calling himself Mierta and men from the kingdom of Vandolay after the Sulchyaes had been murdered. Mierta had threatened him before he suddenly lost consciousness and collapsed to the ground, causing one of the guards to call for Tarik's arrest. Then the rest seemed to be a blur, which probably explained the headache he was currently suffering from as well as what felt like a bloody gash on his forehead. He concluded the guards had beat him into unconsciousness, putting him in the current predicament.

Hearing the sound of other voices, Tarik squinted his eyes as he gazed around the chamber in an attempt to determine his surroundings. He could briefly make out a group of warlocks seated on chairs that seemed to have been carved out of the very walls of the space they were in. There was also another warlock wearing tall black boots, a black tunic with a golden lacing, royal blue breeches and a long-sleeved white linen shirt standing near what appeared to be a large, open area. His face was hidden behind an orange-and-golden mask shaped like a dragon's head. Before Tarik was able to question why he had been brought here or the purpose of the open area, the sound of flapping wings could be heard, and a hot wind filled the room as Lord Kaeto landed in the open area.

They brought me to Draconiera Mountain! My wand? Where is my wand?

Tarik struggled against the restraints, hoping to loosen them in an attempt to successfully manage an escape before the interrogation began.

"It is meaningless to struggle against those restraints. Your wand has been confiscated, and they cannot be undone by your hands," Dragomir said.

"Argh!" Tarik cried with frustration as he tried a little harder against the restraints.

Dragomir turned to Lord Kaeto and nodded.

"*Ventin mortales!*" Lord Kaeto said.

Suddenly, Tarik let out a scream when it felt like his body had been ignited.

"I gather you're comfortable. Yes, I reckon that's enough for now," Dragomir said, raising an eyebrow before looking back at Lord Kaeto for instructions.

Lord Kaeto briefly closed his eyes, allowing the spell to cease.

They watched Tarik take several quick breaths before his pain and breathing started to ease.

"Now, shall we begin?" Dragomir said.

Tarik could feel his heart thumping quickly in his chest and sweat starting to drip down his back. He had never felt such horrific pain in his life. It felt like part of his soul was being burned out of him.

"Tarik Fuller," Dragomir said. "You have been accused of treason for performing a conjuring spell using black magic. What say you?"

"Treason?" Tarik said as if offended. "Why, that's ridiculous. I have done no such thing."

"So, you are denying you conjured up the Sulchyaes, which has resulted in the deaths of several men in the kingdom of Vandolay?"

"Of course not. Those people got what they deserved after their king decided to murder my father," Tarik said.

"And so, you took it upon yourself to leech your revenge upon innocent people?" Dragomir questioned.

"My father was innocent, too!" Tarik shouted.

"I see," Dragomir said. He gazed over to Lord Kaeto, who nodded. "And what about the two warlocks you severely injured?"

"What about them? They got in my way. I would have finished the job if they hadn't interfered."

"Dragomir," Lord Kaeto interrupted. "What have you been told by the healing witches of Poveglia of Mierta?"

"It is my understanding Mierta's been put into a healing sleep, my lord. The witch, Liliana, has assured me he will make a full recovery."

"Very well. You may proceed."

Dragomir removed from his pocket a rolled-up piece of parchment, which was then unrolled before being read aloud.

"The practice of the black arts is strictly forbidden by any witch or warlock residing in the kingdom of Aracelly when it is used for the sole purpose of deliberately causing harm to others. Any witch or warlock found to be practicing such treasonous acts will be immediately subject to the Rite of Abnegation."

Once Dragomir finished, he rerolled the scroll and placed it back into the pocket of his robe.

Tarik could feel his heart thumping quickly again in his chest. He wouldn't permit them to take his magic! He struggled against the restraints again only to realise that he was trapped.

"You have no right to do this to me!" he screamed at Lord Kaeto and Dragomir. "I am a warlock of the kingdom of Aracelly! I will not allow you to turn me into a Magulia!"

Lord Kaeto raised his head. "Tarik Fuller…"

At that moment, Tarik knew he was stuck as he gripped the chair that was keeping him captive.

"I, Lord Kaeto, the first of my name, sentence you to the Rite of Abnegation. You shall be separated from your wand for all eternity and your magical powers shall be eradicated."

"No!" Tarik screamed in terror. "This is not possible! This cannot be happening!"

"*Ventin mortales!*" Lord Kaeto roared.

Tarik let out a long, loud shriek as every inch of his body felt like it was burning, only this time the burning did not stop until he lost consciousness.

CHAPTER NINETEEN

THE KINGDOM OF VANDOLAY
1248 CE

A few weeks later, Lochlann stared at Mierta, who sat on the edge of the seat across from him looking through the window of the carriage door. He had been attempting to rest while on the return journey to the McKinnon estate, but the noise of the horse's hooves clomping along the hardened earth and the uneven dirt road they were travelling on was making it impossible.

Lochlann grimaced as the carriage went over another set of ruts in the ground.

Mierta glanced back at his brother and crinkled his brow in concern, observing the pained expression on his face. "I still have some of the tincture I brought from home. It will help you relax and ease your pain."

"I'm fine," Lochlann answered, watching Mierta search through his satchel for the flask.

"Lochlann," Mierta said, retrieving the remedy. "You, my brother, are a terrible liar."

If they had been anywhere else, Mierta would have responded with a smile and a wink, as the moment reminded him of when he tried to convince his father he was fine after waking in his sickbed. Except this time, their father was up front guiding the horse and carriage, so Mierta would have to be the adult. He unfastened the cap on the flask and handed it over to Lochlann.

"Drink it, but only a sip. It's stronger than it looks," Mierta cautioned.

Lochlann obeyed and handed the flask back to his brother. He then laid back against his seat.

"Are you warm enough?" Mierta asked, adjusting a blanket the castle staff had provided them.

"Yes, I'm fine," Lochlann said. He looked at his brother with worry. "What about you?"

"Me? Oh, no need to be concerned," Mierta said, shaking his right arm around. "See? The warlocks of Poveglia fixed me all up. I'm good as new. Was a bit of touch and go, I reckon, before they put me into their healing sleep or whatever they call it."

"How did you manage to kill it?" Lochlann asked with curiosity.

"I...I don't know, actually," Mierta said, looking down toward the ground with a smile, recalling how his Mum had spoken to him. He did not want to upset his brother so he chose not to tell him this. "I remember one moment I was looking at the creature, realising my life was about to be over, and then the next, I said the words that came to me in the moment."

"Yes? What were the words?"

Mierta looked up at Lochlann with a shocked look. "*Petrosani pan war.* It turned the creature to stone. It was in the air, so it dropped to the ground and shattered into dust."

That was when Lochlann noticed a familiar look on his brother's face, which frightened him.

Mierta noticed his brother had suddenly gone pale. "What? What is it? Why are you looking at me like that? Blimey, Lochlann, I would dare say you look like you've seen a ghost."

It was in that instant that Lochlann recalled the final moments of his Rite of Wands ceremony, where he had first learned of his terrifying fate. In his future, there had been a warlock who strangely reminded him of Mierta, with his short brown hair styled in a similar way. They were in what looked like a run-down castle, though he couldn't identify which castle it was. There, they had argued, which resulted in a warlock duel and, in the end, his death. This warlock had killed him.

Lochlann had believed he could escape this event by refusing to practice magic. However, he was beginning to understand a warlock's role was much more than merely being able to perform magic.

"It's nothing." Lochlann shivered. "It's that only for a moment, you reminded me of someone…in my future."

"Your future?" Mierta asked, puzzled. His eyes widened with understanding. "You mean something you saw in your Rite of Wands?"

"Yes." Lochlann nodded.

"Then, what happened to you back there with the Sulchyaes, you didn't see that event happen before?"

Lochlann shook his head.

"Blimey! Now, quit gawking and scoot over," Mierta said, taking a seat beside him. He placed his hand over the blanket on Lochlann's legs and stared at his brother intently. "Before you say anything more, I must warn you that speaking about your individual Rite of Wands to anyone is forbidden."

"Yes, I know, but I'm…" Lochlann stuttered. "I'm frightened."

Mierta nodded. "Yes, I know, but why?" He paused, his mind racing to come up with some explanation. "Blimey! Is this because I defeated Tarik and killed the Sulchyaes? Are you indicating I do something in the future that scares people?"

"No, no, or at least I reckon not," Lochlann said between a yawn as the remedy was starting to take effect. "Mierta, what you did back in the kingdom of Vandolay was heroic. You saved my life. I will forever be in your debt. Only, you are better than me. You're better than me in a lot of things. That is why I do not feel it fair to ask you…"

"Ask me what?" Mierta said, concerned when Lochlann hesitated.

Learning to master magic and become wittier like Mierta was no longer a choice. It would be required in order to save his life in the future if such events should come to pass. While there still was no guarantee that his destiny would change, perhaps it would be exactly enough to prevent the tall, brown-haired warlock he saw in his Rite of Wands from striking him down when the time came for them to finally face each other in a duel.

"I need you to teach me how to use magic. I need to learn how to duel."

Note from the Author

Thank you for spending your time reading the second book in The Rite of Wands series. If you are brand new to the series, welcome! And if you're picking up from the last book, thank you for your patience between books!

If you enjoyed this book, the greatest compliment you can show an author is by leaving a review. So, would you please leave a short review on your favourite online retail site?

Thank you!

If you would like to be notified of upcoming books and news, please visit my publisher's website at *www.bhcpress.com.*

ACKNOWLEDGMENTS

To Donna Lutkus-Phillips for being my awesome assistant at book signings, my sound board when I'm writing, and especially, a companion when I'm on the road.

To my amazing editors, Lisa McNeilley and Rebecca Rue, for your continual insightful knowledge, feedback, and leadership to help bring my vision to life.

To Doctor Who Online for connecting me with the right people!

To Chris Walker-Thomson for bringing my characters to life in audio and for putting up with some very ridiculous nonsense.

To Steven Morris for designing digital images of my characters in order to show potential clients the complete package.

To my publisher BHC Press, you are the absolute best!

To British actor Matt Smith for your and your family's continual support, inspiration, and for being the voice in my head that never goes away. (That sounds really awkward and weird, but you know what I mean, I think! God help me if it doesn't make sense.)

ABOUT THE AUTHOR

Mackenzie Flohr is the multi-award-winning author of the popular young adult fantasy series The Rite of Wands. A storyteller at heart, she loves to inspire the imagination.

Her previously published works include *The Rite of Wands*, *The Rite of Abnegation*, *The Binge Watcher's Guide to Doctor Who: A History Of Doctor Who And The First Female Doctor*, and her short stories appear in the anthology collections *The Whispered Tales of Graves Grove* and *Unknown Realms*. She is an in-demand speaker at conferences and conventions. Mackenzie makes her home in Mount Morris, Michigan, where she is currently penning her next adventure.

For more information, visit Mackenzie at *www.bhcpress.com* and *www.mackenzieflohr.com*.

CPSIA information can be obtained
at www.ICGtesting.com
Printed in the USA
FSHW012309270921
85002FS